"Did You Like The Way I Kissed You Just Now?"

Salty asked Felicia.

"No."

He was stunned. He drew in a breath of anguish.

"You're much too skilled," she said. "When women are trying to keep their honor, men like you come along and scramble their brains until they're helpless."

"I'm not that good."

"Why am I on your lap?"

"I find that I can't stand up and kiss you at the same time. Kissing you takes all my attention. I want you."

"No."

"You like playing with fire."

She ran her hands across his chest. "Are you fire?"

Dear Reader,

Just when you thought Mother Nature had turned up the heat, along comes Silhouette Desire to make things even *hotter*. It's June...the days are longer, the kids are out of school, and we've got the very best that romance has to offer.

Let's start with our *Man of the Month, Haven's Call,* which is by Robin Elliott, a writer many of you have written to tell me is one of your favorites.

Next, we have *Salty and Felicia* by Lass Small. If you've ever wondered how those two older Browns got together, well, now you'll get to find out! From Jennifer Greene comes the latest installment in her JOCK'S BOYS series, *Bewildered*. And Suzanne Simms's series, HAZARDS, INC., continues with *The Pirate Princess*.

Anne Marie Winston has created a tender, wonderful story, *Substitute Wife*. And if you like drama and intensity with your romance, don't miss Lucy Gordon's *Uncaged!*

It just doesn't get any better than this...so read and enjoy.

All the best,

Lucia Macro
Senior Editor

Please address questions and book requests to:
Reader Service
U.S.: P.O. Box 1325, Buffalo, NY 14269
Canadian: P.O. Box 1050, Niagara Falls, Ont. L2E 7G7

LASS SMALL
SALTY AND FELICIA

SILHOUETTE *Desire*®
Published by Silhouette Books
America's Publisher of Contemporary Romance

SILHOUETTE BOOKS

ISBN 0-373-05860-8

SALTY AND FELICIA

Copyright © 1994 by Lass Small

Printed in U.S.A.

Books by Lass Small

Silhouette Desire

Tangled Web #241
To Meet Again #322
Stolen Day #341
Possibles #356
Intrusive Man #373
To Love Again #397
Blindman's Bluff #413
Goldilocks and the Behr #437
Hide and Seek #453
Red Rover #491
Odd Man Out #505
Tagged #534
Contact #548
Wrong Address, Right Place #569
Not Easy #578
The Loner #594
Four Dollars and Fifty-One Cents #613
No Trespassing Allowed #638
The Molly Q #655
+*'Twas the Night* #684
Dominic #697
+*A Restless Man* #731
+*Two Halves* #743
+*Beware of Widows* #755
A Disruptive Influence #775
+*Balanced* #800
+*Tweed* #817
+*A New Year* #830
+*I'm Gonna Get You* #848
+*Salty and Felicia* #860

Silhouette Romance

An Irritating Man #444
Snow Bird #521

Silhouette Books

Silhouette Christmas Stories 1989
"Voice of the Turtles"
Silhouette Spring Fancy 1993
"Chance Encounter"

*Lambert Series
+Fabulous Brown Brothers

LASS SMALL

finds living on this planet at this time a fascinating experience. People are amazing. She thinks that to be a teller of tales of people, places and things is absolutely marvelous.

To the network of do-ers who led me to
Diann Shappell in Fort Wayne, who referred
me along to the Merrick House in Cleveland,
and to John Noga.
Thank you all for your information and kindness.

One

Since he smoked those awful big black cigars, Ray had been banished to the far back of the Browns' mowed yard where he was out of contact with civilized people. He wasn't an actual or adopted child or even a sometime visitor of the Browns. He was an in-law. When he wasn't smoking these smelly weeds, he was well liked.

Gradually some of the other men drifted back and sat with the exile. It was dusk, there in Temple, Ohio, just south of Cleveland. The early summer night was alive with the excitement of new growth, so it wasn't surprising when those isolated males' lazy talk turned to sex.

It started with a joke. In the male misusage of ordinary words, few women would have understood how vulgar it was. To men, innocent words have another meaning altogether.

One remark led to another, and Salty's first adopted child, Rod, remembered, "The first time I really understood sex, I was hiding and watching Salty and Felicia."

There were verbal chuffing blats of disbelief.

Rod was serious. "What I'm really talking about is making love. Watching them, I understood the difference between having sex and making love."

They all snorted and laughed at Rod.

Rod shook his head with slow patience. "You still don't understand. It wasn't dirty, it was a...sharing. After that, I knew that sex was more than an act. That it was beautiful."

Cray dismissed Rod's revelation. "Dad always told us that."

Mike put in, "Yeah, but hearing and understanding aren't always synonymous."

Bob asked John, "Did you know Mike knew that word?"

"He's sly," John replied. "He has a whole 'nother vocabulary past us'uns."

In his usual calm, Mitchell observed, "He's Army. He knows more than he's ever allowed us to realize."

Mike snorted.

Saul was eighteen. He felt old enough to add, "Mike married a schoolteacher. She uses big words."

Rod nodded. "That might explain 'synonymous.' But he did know when to use it. That's progress."

Mitchell lay back in his yard chair and commented in a reminiscing manner, "I watched how Salty handled Felicia, and it made me understand patience. A man can be thrilled right out of his skin if he's just patient enough with a woman."

"Yeah." Tweed looked off at the fading color of the sunset. "I learned to allow the woman to flirt back."

Ray blew out another cloud of stench. "Did you, now."

"Well." Tweed did try not to smile. "About every third time."

Sometime Brown child, Harry Mentor, put in soberly, "When I came back home after the first Christmas, I knew I'd made a big mistake in marrying a contentious woman. That's why I divorced the first one."

John referred to their parents, "They've had such an easy life. They match so perfectly."

Tom shook his head in compassion for their parents. "Think of being thirty-eight years old and the muscle for a stage show and having to see an eighteen-year-old Felicia in a satin sliplike thing—every night."

With such confidence, Tweed was sure, "Salty could handle it."

In a dreamy way, John said, "I remember when Salty came home with those stinky lilies and said..."

In Cleveland, Ohio, the home of the Cleveland Indians, the year was 1962. People watched Ed Sullivan, Perry Como and "Show of Shows."

Men wore cardigan sweaters, golf shirts and pleated trousers, and they wore loafer shoes.

Women wore sheath dresses, which skimmed their bodies loosely, and their gloves were wrist length. They wore pillbox hats.

John Kennedy was president. John Glenn had orbited the earth three times in February. And John Noga had just opened his floral shop in the city's neighborhood called Tremont.

At that time the helpful Merrick House had been in the Tremont section of Cleveland for over thirty years.

It was the florist, John Noga, who told Salty, "They need a man who can take off his shirt onstage. Why don't you volunteer?"

Salty was a little startled. His fight-ring voice rasped logically, "Why?"

"The navy worked you so hard that you have the body. They need some muscle to stand around onstage."

Salty snorted as he paid for the bouquet of lilies.

"Why not?" John Noga didn't look at Salty. He was trimming some fern to go with the roses.

"I never had any ambition to stand around on a stage. I got better things to do."

John turned from his bouquet and scanned his customer. Salty was tall enough. He was built like a bulldog. All shoulders, no hips. He had an ear that had been hit too many times. His voice box had been abused in the ring. His good nose had somehow survived the batterings. His thick, black hair waved slightly but tended to be untidy. He had a heavy beard that didn't darken his face because his skin was so weatherworn. His brows were straight and level as his gaze.

John turned back to his work as he said, "Just show up and volunteer. You can meet some new people. Those boys you adopted would be expanded. You can get involved in the community. Be a good citizen."

Salty asked, "How come you know about what they want?"

"One of the cast members lives near here. She's the ingenue."

Salty said in disgust, "An innocent. I don't need that complication in my life."

"You want an old, settled woman," Noga guessed.

Salty squinted. "Well, there must be something in between."

They were both silent. Then as the florist put the roses and ferns together perfectly, he suggested again, "Why not go down and volunteer? You might make a contact. However..." He paused. "I don't know very many women who would want to start out with three kids."

"My boys are the epitome of good manners."

"Yeah. I'll give them that... when you're around."

Salty looked at the busy florist. "You telling me they misbehave?"

"Now, Salty, you know better. You terrify them."

Salty was shocked. "Do you mean when I threaten them with mayhem, they take it... seriously?"

Admiring his vase of roses, Noga shook his head. "Salty Brown, you're a pushy man."

His rasp was worse, "I never realized that! I thought I was a Caspar Milquetoast."

The florist laughed as Salty patted his shoulder on the way out of the shop.

None of the boys liked the lilies. They stunk. Salty told them, "Nothing stinks like men who haven't bathed during a five-day storm when everybody works their tails off to keep the ship afloat while they sweat out the gale."

"Yeah." Rod was the eldest and almost nine. Salty was just thirty-eight. The other two boys were younger than Rod. They'd been with Salty for just over three years.

The middle boy, Mike, suggested, "Let's give the lilies a bath."

"I'm trying to teach you guys couth."

"Couth?" They puzzled over that one.

"You know uncouth, so now I'm teaching you couth. Couth people have flowers in their houses."

"Not lilies." John was sure.

So Salty took the flowers over to the lady next door, who went into a flutter of excitement. Salty had to then explain that the boys didn't like the smell of lilies. Then he explained about being couth. Finally he asked if she wanted him to give the flowers to someone else.

Disappointed in him, she agreed that he should give them to someone else. Salty couldn't face returning the beautiful flowers, so he gave them to a stranger, who was very surprised and quite pleased. Salty said, "Those are a gift from John Noga, the new florist."

After that, the lady next door declined to sit with Salty's boys. While his sons were exuberant, Salty was disgruntled. So Salty took the three boys along to the theater to see why he should volunteer to be onstage.

Salty told the three, "You'll get to see how a play is organized. You'll learn what it's like to be an actor, and how it is for people to practice being in a play. They call it rehearsing. Doing something over and over until it is just right and you remember."

By then, the boys were smart enough to be noncommittal. To show enthusiasm for something unknown generally turned out to be something stupid. They went along quietly.

Seated in the back of the unlit theater, the Browns looked at the big, empty stage on which the actors, in various dress, sat on wooden ice-cream parlor chairs or folding steel ones. They read from scripts. It was droning, reading and talking and discussing, without gestures or emotion.

The three little boys looked around at the empty seats, up at the balcony, and they hissed in stage whispers. That meant loud steam blasts. "Can we go look?"

Salty replied, "Stay on this floor, don't go outside... and be quiet. No running or fighting."

That was reasonable.

Salty stared at the stage. He'd picked out the ingenue immediately and was riveted by her. She was probably sixteen or seventeen, an—as yet—unformed siren. She was too young for him. In ten years she'd be an uncontrollable, knowledgeable vixen and all men who paused to look at her would be ruined forever.

While Salty glanced at the other people on the stage— and noted the two men who weren't interested in the vixen—his eyes were drawn back to her as if they were steel bits and she was a magnet. He felt he was fortunate to realize the danger of her right away. He could avoid that pitfall.

She had great eyes with incredible eyelashes. Her face was mostly eyes. They looked into a man's soul. She looked out at him and stared in rapture. Sure. He knew full well that from the footlighted stage, she could not see anyone in the chairs. She couldn't even tell if anyone was there.

Since she couldn't know his interest, he felt safe from her. While he could look and fill his soul with the looking, she would be unaware of his regard.

She had medium dark hair. For the 1960s it was long and unfashionable. Long, soft hair. It was naturally wavy. A man could wrap his hand in all that hair and hold her head steady as he ravished her mouth with his own.

Salty shifted in the seat. He looked away from her and breathed with careful discipline. He was still in control.

She had the complexion that made a woman a killer. Her cool, pale skin looked as if it would be warm to the touch. A man could be driven to all sorts of ploys just to see if that was true. He would have to search to find where she would be warm, and where she might be too hot.

She'd be a terror in a couple of years, when she'd gotten enough experience with men and realized what slaves they would all be... to her. For her.

Salty probably would have escaped her in time, but John, the youngest, who was just past five, went up on the stage. Salty had said to stay on the first floor and not go outside, but he hadn't said anything about not going onstage. John wanted to see the pretty lady closer. He went and stood in front of her so that he could look his fill.

She smiled at the child.

The other adults looked on patiently. The stage director looked around to see who was responsible for the kid.

Felicia said, with her throaty voice lightened, "Well, hello." And she smiled.

Salty was rising from his seat to fetch his child, when he saw the other two following after John. All three lined up before the siren.

The stage manager put his arm below his eyes to block the footlights, and he squinted as he asked, "Somebody out there responsible for these kids?"

And Salty's raspy voice said, "Yeah."

Just the sound of the voice from the audience shivered the skin on Felicia's back, peaked her nipples and caused her lips to part as she gasped a breath.

Rod asked her solemnly, "You cold?" He was not quite nine years old.

But she was trying to see beyond the children.

Salty's rasp suggested, "Come on down, boys."

John walked to the footlights and stretched out his neck, moving his head and trying to see. "You out there, Dad?"

"Yeah."

"I can't see you. You disappeared." A good word for a kid just barely five.

It was so still on the stage that they could hear the carpeted footsteps coming down toward the stage. After hearing the bodiless voice, and then the male footsteps, some of the men got agitated. The stage manager called, "Spike?"

"Yo!"

"You watching?"

"No problem."

And Salty appeared in the light near the steps, to one side. "Come along, boys."

"Hey," the director said suddenly, "You from the Tremont neighborhood? John Noga told me about you. Come on up here."

Salty hesitated. He said, "Well, I don't think—"

"Take off your jacket."

Salty was appalled. "Well, you see—"

The director went toward Salty, talking the entire time. "I'm Joe Baker. I've been appointed director for this particular presentation. We need some muscle. You don't have to say a word. I heard you talking. Does that hurt?"

Salty shook his head, speechless. He sneaked a look at the girl. She was watching him. John was leaning against her knees and holding her hand on her lap. Salty would probably have to keep an eye on John until he was safely married. Already John was holding her hand! How'd he manage that?

Joe urged, "Come on up on the stage, and let's get a look at you. If that isn't all padding, you might do!"

Salty stalled, "I just have to get the boys—"

"No problem. Boys, you go to Phyllis over there, yeah. Phyllis, would you please take the boys off over to the side and give them something to do? Maybe they could sort out the flags?" He turned back to Salty. "Come along. Let's see what we've got here."

If she hadn't been there watching with those big eyes, Salty could have handled it. But she rattled him. She had to be half his age, anyway, and she could do something like that to a retired sailor? Think of it!

He moved slowly up the stairs and stepped onto the stage, prowling like the battered alley cat he was. She was still watching him. He narrowed his eyes down as he walked toward her, and when he was within the exact distance for her to hear, his injured voice growled softly, "Does your mother know you're out after dark?"

Her eyes sparkled and she replied in her lightened, deep Talullah Bankhead voice, "I gave her permission to stay out a little later."

He considered her. "You're one of those."

She tilted her head and lifted her chin as she smiled very, very faintly—and snubbed him.

Middle son Mike was there. He covered her hand on her lap and explained, "He's all bluff."

She laughed a low, throaty sound.

Salty tightened his mouth and took a patient breath. They'd garnered the attention of the gathered people who had listened and then laughed.

Mike was serious. His look challenged his adoptive father.

Salty's rusty voice said, "Mike, she appreciates you. Go help your brothers."

Mike nodded obediently, but he told the ingenue, "Call me if you need me." He was seven.

Joe said, "Take it off!" and clapped his hands as his grin became real. So the others picked it up, clapping and chanting, "Take it off!"

Somebody went over to the piano and began to play a really dirty version of "The Stripper" with a good, thudding bass. Wicked.

What was Salty to do? He took off his jacket in a smooth, ordinary way. He resisted allowing them to lead him along into showing off. He'd been tempted. He'd have liked stripping for her, but not in front of other people. Not with his kids there. He flicked a glance over to her. She watched.

He stood still, holding his jacket in one hand along his side. He pretended to be just an ordinary guy. The man at the piano quit with a flourish and turned to watch. The bunch applauded, laughing.

Joe whistled softly and exclaimed, "You're real! We need you in an undershirt. Will you take off the shirt? We want to see you."

His kids were busy. She watched him, and his ego took over. He knew he looked good. He pulled his shirt out from his trousers and began to unbutton it.

Phyllis called, "Need any help?"

And other women said, "Let me!"

But the nubile woman sat and just watched. She narrowed her eyes down a little and didn't miss a twitch.

He had to distract himself or he'd be embarrassed. He looked over at the boys who were busily sorting through colors. They would have to go home soon. This would be over. He shrugged the shirt off his shoulder and

pulled the sleeve from his arm. He did the other and
stood—bare chested.

The men whistled softly in envy, the women squealed
and clapped. She didn't do anything. She sat and looked
him over. Her attention on him was very erotic for Salty.
He lifted his hand, partway, to move the screening shirt
in front of his susceptible crotch.

Joe was asking, "Ever had any experience doing
plays?"

"A little."

"What'd you do?"

"I played a spear carrier." In the navy, he'd been in
several plays including *Death of a Salesman* and *Front
Page*.

Joe was coaxing. "There aren't any lines. You just
have to react. The guy's a mute."

"With my voice box, that would be about right." He
bit into his busy tongue. That had sounded as if he was
considering being in the play.

"Your rusty voice would be good. But could you carry
any dialogue? Would your voice fade?"

His tongue wouldn't stop. "No. I can yell at guys for
a long time. It doesn't change." And he knew he was
talking to her.

"It sounds like it's about to go out."

His libido went right on, taking over, replying for him.
"I've won a lot of shouting contests between guys."

Joe laughed. "I'd bet you didn't need your voice."

Hastily, for her benefit, he urged, "Actually, I'm not
at all hostile. I'm not a physical man." He was appalled! He'd said that to make her feel she had nothing
to fear from him. Why would he care if she was fearful
of him? There would never be a test. His independent,
undisciplined eyes stole a quick look at her.

She was watching his face with those big eyes. A man could drown in those eyes. My God, he shouldn't be anywhere around her. She was lethal. He began to put his shirt back on. The women protested, and the men laughed.

Joe said, "We need you. You're just right. The salary is no problem, we don't pay anything. But it'll be fun. The kids can be busy. We never stay past nine-thirty ea—"

There were blats of derisions.

Joe protested, "Now, haven't I told you a hundred times we won't be longer than nine-thirty?"

And a male voice replied, "You tell us that every night—about ten-thirty."

Joe was astonished. "We've stayed later than nine-thirty?"

There were catcalls and snorts and more rude noises.

Salty said, "The boys are young. I need to get them home."

Joe coaxed, "School's out. Let 'em sleep later tomorrow."

"They've had a long day. They'll get cantankerous, and I'm too fragile to have to step in and stop a fight."

Everybody laughed. Salty smiled.

Felicia never took her serious stare off him.

It's unsettling for a grown man who has discarded knowing a budding woman to be the interest of her evaluation. He wanted to move his body and look back. He didn't dare. He was spending all his energy in avoiding looking back and in controlling his libido . . . trying to control it.

His sex hadn't been this eager, uninvited, in a long time. He pulled on his shirt and left the screening shirt-tails outside his trousers as he told Joe, "I don't think this is a good idea. Good luck on the search. There're a lot of guys that look better than—me." He'd almost said "I." He didn't want to seem too smooth.

There was a primarily female protest, and the guys laughed in mock protest over the women's response to Salty.

Salty called to the boys, "Come along. It's past...nine-thirty." He looked at Joe.

Joe looked at his watch and rather elaborately lifted it to his ear to listen, and then he shook it. He complained, "It musta stopped."

The cast hooted.

Phyllis told Salty, "We're almost done."

The boys hesitated, smiled at Salty and went back to sorting.

Salty pushed his arms into the sleeves of his jacket as he asked Joe, "What're the flags for?"

"Storage. Kids. Punishment for recalcitrant actresses."

"Ahh."

Joe chuckled. "I'd like you around. If you don't want the part, come around, anyway. You're refreshingly lacking in ego."

Salty denied that. "It's the weight of my ego that kept me from jumping up onto the stage flatfooted."

Joe swatted Salty's shoulder. "I'll let them go tonight, and we'll get a beer and talk."

"You'll have to come home with me. The boys need to get to bed."

"Okay." Then he told the cast, "That's all for tonight. Seven *sharp!* Be here tomorrow. Hear me?"

"Yeah, yeah," came the humorously impatient voices. "We hear you." "That's all you ever say."

"And we quit at nine-thirty," another added.

The director spoke in a brilliantly penetrating voice, "Memorize your lines. Pay attention. Read your scripts. If you plan to be in this play, you have to know your lines."

There were impatient responses that were minimal and automatic as the cast members gathered their things.

Joe had his own car. Salty gave Joe their address. Joe said he knew the Tremont area. So Salty gathered his sons and herded them out of there.

He resisted looking back at the lure of her. It took iron discipline. He was proud of himself. Then he remembered: Pride goeth before a fall.

In the Tremont area, the Brown house was modest. It was two story and a rental. Salty was looking around at schools and neighborhoods. The house had four bedrooms upstairs, with two baths. It was an old house. The old sewing room had been converted into the second bath for the biggest bedroom. Their collection of furniture was sparse. The beds were all new.

Salty left the front door ajar with a note, "Joe, come on in."

Then he herded his boys upstairs and put all three into the filled tub in the larger bathroom. The three shared the biggest bedroom.

Salty growled, "Don't splash. Understand?"

Mike complained, "Rod has more room than me."

Salty corrected, "I."

"Aye. He's got more room."

Salty corrected, "He has more room."

Mike complained, "That's what I said."

Rod put in, "You said, 'got' more."

Mike said, "Move."

Rod replied, "Make me."

Salty rasped, "I will."

"Aw, Dad, you take everything serious."

"Yep." He was sitting on the closed toilet lid, supervising.

Downstairs, Joe hollered, "I'm here."

Salty stood up and went to the bathroom door. "Beer's in the refrigerator."

"Right. Smart."

Salty grinned at the boys. "Hurry up. Hit the deck. Look alive."

He helped the youngest boy, John, who was capable of taking care of himself, but he was slow.

"Brush your teeth."

There were varying agreeing replies or grunts of acknowledgment.

Salty said, "Good night. I'll see you in the morning. Mike, it's your night to see to it that everything's shipshape. You're in charge. Got that?"

"Yeah."

"How's that?"

"Yes, sir."

"I'll be up to check. Behave."

"G'night."

"You're great guys. I was lucky to find you."

"Aw, Salty..."

"See you in the morning." He hugged each one and left them. He went down the stairs, and there was Joe all right. But with him was...she. The ingenue.

Good God, why had Joe dragged her along? To tempt him into being in that stupid play? Walking around in an undershirt? Seeing her every single damned night? No way.

Salty was formally cordial and his glances at Joe were cool. He said to the water witch, "I don't believe we've been introduced. I'm Salty Brown."

Her marvelously manipulative voice replied, "I'm Felicia Strode."

They were very conscious of one another.

Joe loved it. He sprawled and talked and gestured as if he was a prized guest. He'd gotten a beer. Then like a cherished friend, he'd gone through the cabinets and found a special bottle of wine which he'd opened, and she was sipping it. Was she old enough to drink wine?

Salty frowned. A minor drinking his wine could put him in jail, couldn't it? He asked her, "How old are you?"

She moved her head slowly, lifted her eyebrows just a tad and looked at him with those enormous eyes. She asked, "Does a gentleman inquire a lady's age?"

"If the death squad forbids minors' drinking, he does."

"I'm eighteen." She said it kindly.

"Got any proof?"

"You could cut off my leg and count the rings?"

Joe prevented Salty's blood pressure from going to overload. He said in a pushing-away-an-annoyance tone, "She's actually over eighteen."

Salty looked at her with clear eyes. "Two days?"

"Last December." She gentled her rich voice as one does who speaks to an idiot.

With her attitude, it was a good thing that Salty had already discarded her.

TWO

Joe sat back in the corner of the sofa—relaxed, smiling—as he listened to the stilted, hostile exchange between the two fascinating people who were of the opposite sex. It was like watching the end of a first act.

Salty moved like a large, dangerous cat as he swung his head to look at the almost-woman. She sat rather primly on one of the antique chairs he had taken out of storage. The chair had been in his family for some long time. His mother had called it a formal ladies' chair, because, on it, a woman couldn't sit any other way.

The chair was walnut, and the wood was carved with tiny flower indentations. The middle of the back, the forearm part of the chair arms and the seat were covered with needlepoint. It was not a comfortable chair. It was too formal. It suited the budding woman sitting on it, right then.

Unwittingly, Salty thought she looked good in that chair. She was an elegant lady. That low voice of hers was a surprise. It went with her big eyes and her...beauty.

She was a beauty. A budding one. But...she handled herself well. For being as young as she was, she did handle herself like a pro. A pro. Unfortunately, her profession wasn't a sexual one. Had it been, he could have solved his fascination without becoming involved.

He asked her, "How do you make your living?" And he waited for her reply.

"I'm still in school." Her face was courteous. She would have gotten away with her reply, but her voice betrayed her slight irony.

He couldn't resist. "Junior high?"

She lied with easy assurance. "I've been held back."

Joe har-dee-har-har-harred.

Salty gave the siren a patient look, but he couldn't just continue to stare. He had to tear his eyes from her so he did see the three standing in the entrance hall, watching the witch.

He asked the threesome, "Why aren't you in bed?"

"We wanted to tell Felicia good-night."

Salty glanced at her. She had turned her head and smiled gently at the boys. She said, "Good night."

Although it was early summer, they grinned their best Christmas smiles and responded as if each one was the sole recipient of her attention. They said a chorused, "Good night."

She said nothing else. She didn't encourage them any further. She turned her face from them, confident her brief words were all they wanted.

Salty observed his dismissed sons. They smiled at each other, and they said a barely audible good-night to the

other two bodies in the living room as they disappeared
from sight. Their bare feet rumbled up the now thickly
carpeted stairs, and their door slammed.

Salty glanced tellingly at Joe and shared. "Even kids
that age."

"You ought to've seen the fossils at the nursing home
last Christmas. She rejuvenated them."

That response allowed Salty to turn his attention to the
vixen. She was giving Joe a patient look that would
shrivel most men. Joe laughed. He wasn't shrivelable.

She sipped the last of her very small glass of wine.

Salty asked with some uncalled-for tolerance, "You
driving?"

"No."

He turned his head to Joe.

Joe shrugged. "Her car's—uh—what was it you
said?" He looked at one Cause of All Trouble.

She supplied the word. "It's being difficult."

Salty immediately offered, "I could bend it for you."

And she smiled a little as she said, "Yes."

Joe watched sleepily as Salty told her gently, "I can fix
any motor. Want me to look at it for you?"

"What do you charge?"

As if he was considering his reply, Salty looked down
her and back up. He said in his gravelly voice, "The first
time's free."

Then Salty moved as if awakening, and he frowned as
he shifted his feet. He said, "Want another beer?" to
Joe.

Joe said, "Naw. I've got to go. My old lady will be
waiting up to be sure I get home all right."

"Your... mother?"

Joe grinned. "My wife."

Salty almost nodded. He still hadn't sat down. He was still standing around and unaware of it.

Joe stood up and told Felicia, "You can walk from here." Then he said to Salty, "Come tomorrow night. We need you."

Salty witnessed Joe leave. Joe just walked on out the door and went out to his car, started it and drove away!

And there she sat. That nubile woman who was a siren. What in bloody hell was he supposed to do with her? All sorts of ideas crowded for his attention.

The silence stretched. She considered him. He avoided doing anything but watch his feet and try to control all automatic, urgent and uncivilized impulses.

In his rough voice, he said gently, "You sit on that chair like a princess."

She moved her fingers on the carved, ornate ends of the chair's arms. "It's a marvelous chair. We have a similar one."

Lightening his rasp, he said, "I wish I was young enough for you."

"I hadn't realized I'd given you any indication that I was interested."

"I beg your pardon."

"There's no need. It is redundant."

"Shall I call a cab for you?"

"I live just a few blocks down the alley."

He was appalled and felt besieged. "That close?"

"How far do you want me to walk?"

He studied her large eyes and her maddening mouth. He told her honestly in his lightened rasp, "On the other side of the world."

"As I understand, that world is upside down, and I would be upside down there, and my blood would all go to my head and my hair would stand on end."

"That's why we have gravity."

"Oh. I've heard of that!" Her marvelous voice gave no indication of surprise, so her exclamation was droll-ness, chiding him for rejecting her and trying to treat her as he would a child.

Softening his rough voice, he said, "I'm old enough to be your father."

She rose from her chair and went to him. "And I'm old enough." With that, she turned away, went across the room and out the front door.

He caught her as she went down the front steps. "You can't walk home alone."

"Why?"

"This is a big city. Big cities are dangerous for young girls. You can't walk alone after dark."

"I'm only a couple of blocks from my house. I know everyone in this area. I walk all over everywhere, all the time. It isn't dangerous. You're hyper." She released her arm from his big hands and started off again.

He followed her in the dark, across the lawn.

She looked back at him. "No need for this. Good night."

"You got a driver's license?"

"Of course."

"Then take my car. You can bring it back in the morning. I can't have you walking around this late."

"I'm perfectly all right."

"I don't know that."

"Take my word for it. I walk at night all the time. It's okay."

"Take my car. I'll sleep better. You can drive?" He'd tacked that on belatedly.

She looked at his car. A '62 Chevy Impala convert-ible. It was white with red trim. She peeked inside and saw the red bucket seats, automatic floor shift. A console. How typical, she thought, for a prowling male to have such a car. She said to him, "I told you I have a car. It just doesn't work."

"I can look at it. Can you get it over here tom— You'll have mine. Bring mine back, and I'll go look at yours."

"We'll see."

She took his keys from his palm and her fingers didn't touch his skin as they should have. Disgruntled, he looked at her.

She unlocked his car door and got in. She adjusted the seat and the mirrors. He felt sour. Nobody fooled with his car seat or the mirrors. She did. He'd have to reset them all. Trying to feel discouraged, he watched her drive away from him.

He was thrilled she would be driving his car. She was sitting on his seat. Her hands were on the wheel, her fingers had adjusted everything. Why couldn't she adjust him?

Now from where had that thought popped? It was what he'd been thinking all along. He was a dirty old man. He lusted for an almost-woman. Yeah.

She was too young. He was too old. He'd move.

He stood outside and looked on the quiet night. He could hear televisions going. He could hear radios. Cars went by moderately. He could hear laughter.

He felt alone.

All those years in the navy, he'd never been isolated. Here, in the thriving city of Cleveland, Ohio, he was alone.

The boys didn't count. They were his responsibility.

Instead of having a perfect friend in the area for his retirement, he was out there in a strange city, alone. How had that happened? Fate.

Who'd ever believe a man like George could be hit by a car and killed? His best friend was dead, now, for almost four months. George's wife and kids had moved back to Washington state. He'd seen the last of their things off just a month ago.

And now Salty was being tormented by a woman too young to be a whole woman—yet. Life gets tedious, as his shipmate, Pepper, used to say.

And Salty was irritated to realize he hadn't even asked Felicia where she lived or if she had a last name or anything. He'd just given her the keys to his car and watched her drive it off.

He looked up at God's house and he felt sour. What had his guardian angel been doing this whole evening? Where was he? He'd served Salty very well for all these years, and now when Salty needed him, he was gone.

Guardian angel? Well, he'd told the boys they each had one. He'd told them they weren't to give those overworked spirits too many challenges. Even guardians were limited to what all they could do to save their charges—like George's. Damn. Salty would miss George all the rest of his life.

He walked around his yard and lifted his face to the lake breeze. It felt strange to be in a confined city that not only didn't float but stayed in one place. Would he stay there without George and his family? If he didn't, where would he and the boys go?

Felicia came to his door the next morning and handed Salty his car keys. The boys were exuberant. Salty was stern. She asked, "Are you going to look at my car?"

"Yeah."

The almost nine-year-old Rod asked, "Are you hungry? Come eat."

And without brushing against him at all, she adroitly came past Salty's blocking body, inside his house and followed the noisy, welcoming boys to the kitchen. She was back inside his house. He closed the door slowly, and he was proud that he didn't nail it shut.

What was he thinking!

Sternly, he went back to the kitchen and stood in the doorway. No one there needed anything from him. He watched as the boys welcomed her and made her one of them. They served her. How naturally they managed. They allowed her to choose what she wanted, and they gave up their share without any argument at all.

Salty couldn't believe it. All the while, he'd had to divide everything into thirds with bickering and arguing and hostility, and here those three were, giving in to a not-yet-woman who was older than they. They'd never treated him with such respect or care.

He was jealous . . . of them.

He watched her. She didn't fawn over the boys. She accepted what she wanted and ignored th— No, she was just quiet about it. She maneuvered them. She told them what she expected of them and, like slaves, they did as she wanted.

The boys were under her spell. She was a gypsy woman. She mesmerized any male. She would.

He'd fix her car and not see anything more of her. He'd protect his boys from her lure. And him—he'd protect himself from her. She was a witch.

He said nothing about anything. He listened and he moved and he fixed himself something to eat. He absently put tomorrow's doughnut holes on the table, and she divided them up.

Salty was eating the third one from his share when he realized what he'd done. He'd given her tomorrow's doughnut holes because he'd had nothing else to give her. He'd done that! He was as bad as his sons.

He had to get over to her place and get her car fixed so that he could get rid of her.

She fixed those big eyes on him. She smiled just as if he was the only interesting man she'd ever seen. She said, "I love doughnut holes all squishy and crusty with icing."

He was innovative. He replied, "Yeah."

The boys laughed and chewed and watched her.

Any male would watch her. Salty narrowed his eyes and tried to believe she was mortal and no problem. He was not successful.

His imagination ran with her, taking her to a sea cave and chaining her inside to await his demands. And he would go out and win for her the gems and rings and golden things to decorate her body, her fingers and toes and wrists, her ears.... Her ears were a mortal's ears. They didn't peak or fan. No. They *were* shells. They were intricate shells, and once she had lived in the sea.

How long before she had to return to the sea and again become immortal? Why had she come to him? Why had she assumed human form?

The sea gods probably hadn't forgiven Salty Brown for becoming a landlocked landlubber. This female was their revenge. Their lure to get him back. How long could she walk on land before her legs fused back into a mermaid's tail?

"There," she said. "You boys did a good job of clearing things away. Who taught you that?"

"Salty."

"You call him Salty?"

"It's his name." Rod was reasonable.

She asked, "Why don't you call him Dad when you speak to him?"

"We do it either way," Rod replied.

Mike soothed her by adding, "He doesn't care."

"I see." She looked at Salty in a weighing way.

He said, "They'll get around to it. Just being with me has been an adjustment for them. Rod was lonely with just me, so we got Mike and John to help us out. They're good kids."

She gave him the gift of her approving smile. It was like a benediction. He felt she'd approved of him. Now, why should he feel the need of her approval? This kid. He growled, "Let's get your car fixed."

It was then that his youngest, John, soothed Felicia earnestly, "Salty just talks that way. He don't mean to scare you."

In shock, Salty gasped. He'd been thinking only of her impact on him, not how he was to her. He considered her. She was as confident as a siren five-thousand-years old who'd cut notches in ten thousand trees. He said, "I boxed, and got hit in the throat too many times. This is just the way I talk."

Rod explained, "He scares big dogs just saying 'Git' to them."

It wasn't the first time Salty realized they needed a dog. He hadn't had one in a long, long time. "Where's the dog pound?" he asked the lethal woman.

They went there first. It was a struggle not to adopt more than five. By being severe, Salty kept it to two. One was a collie and nine years old. She had the most beautiful manners. The vet said she probably wouldn't last long, but she did love a family. Her name was Sweetie. Her family had been transferred to the Far East and couldn't take her along. They were relieved to be able to write that family and tell them their dog had been adopted.

Salty made sure the boys were gentle with her.

The other was a large, pleasant male with a pronounced underbite, swirly black hair and a gray beard, who was willing to go anywhere and do anything. All he needed was a clue to what was needed. He wasn't pretty. His name was Mutt. A perfect name.

The boys were exuberant, and the dogs fit into the car with familiarity. Sweetie looked out the window with little interest. Mutt sat on feet or laps and licked faces. The boys laughed.

By then it was lunchtime. The old sailor finally asked the nubile almost-woman, "Did you have anything you needed to do this morning?" It was a rather belated question.

"No."

Salty had loved having her along. He'd managed to touch her waist a couple of times. He'd watched her as she watched the dogs. She was a pushover for dogs. Any dog. She'd touched Sweetie with such gentleness. And the dog loved her.

That's why they'd selected Sweetie. Salty had managed several times to stand close to Felicia, and he was able to glance at her chest as she breathed. He was so tense and hot that he was smothering. He'd had to get his badly needed supply of oxygen through parted lips.

He knew he was tempting a personal disaster. He needed to get away from her so that he could live without grieving for her. As soon as he'd looked at her car and gotten it to run, he'd never see her again.

But they had to have lunch first, and they couldn't take the dogs to a drive-in or buy food there and tempt the dogs. So they went back to the Brown house. He apologized to Felicia.

Did she suggest he just take her home? No. She asked the boys, "What do you want to eat for lunch?"

"Peanut butter."

And she acted surprised. She exclaimed in her subtly deepened voice.

The boys told her that was what they wanted. Mike wanted mustard on his peanut butter. She questioned mustard on peanut butter. Mike assured her it was the only way to eat it.

So, Salty noted, there she was, back in his house.

She organized water dishes for his new dogs, and she settled them in. She had the boys slowly take the dogs around the house and yard to get them acquainted with their new home. She went into Salty's kitchen and opened cupboard doors and looked at his supplies.

She told him, "Your cupboards are bare."

So was his bed. He replied, "I have the fixings for coney dogs."

"All right."

She'd given him permission to make coney dogs for her.

He fixed lunch. She went outside and cut a great armload of daylilies and snowballs for a summer bouquet on their large, round kitchen table. She set it with flair, doing everything just so.

He was charmed by her. How was he to get rid of her?

At lunch, she listened. She noted and paid attention, but only to the boys. She didn't turn those big eyes on Salty and encourage him to tell her what all he wanted to do to her. No. She just listened to the boys who vied for her attention. She told them to hush and eat.

Salty got to control the dogs and make them leave the table. Mutt thought he ought to share a chair with John. John was willing. Salty objected. Felicia observed.

The boys willingly helped to clear the table and load the dishwasher. Felicia did her share. Salty loved watching her bend over and stand up and push back her hair and lick her lips. He loved her interest, her lack of self-consciousness, her being in his house.

It was a mistake having her there. He needed to get her out of his house and back to her own place with a car that worked. He didn't need this temptation. He was too old for her.

He wasn't so old. He wasn't even forty yet. She was too young.

She said, "I know of a lady who is older, who would live here and be with the children. She wouldn't shop or cook or care for others, or for someone ill, nor would she discipline a child. She would call the doctor or the police, and she could monitor whether or not a child should leave the yard. She would want to know where the child would be. Are you interested in her?"

"How old and frail is she?"

"While she lives on a pension, she isn't frail. She would have her bridge club here. Most of the ladies live in rooms or apartments or with family, and to come to a house would be nice. Do you have bridge tables? Card tables? Enough chairs?"

"What would she do with her time?"

"She reads and talks on her own phone line. You'd have to see to that. She writes letters. She would wait for you to fix the meals. She would do her own laundry. Not yours."

"I could interview her."

"Her name is Anne Thompson." She took a sheet from his grocery list and wrote the name, address and phone number.

"How old is she?"

"I've never asked."

"Is she looking for a husband?"

"No."

"I could interview her," he repeated, nodding slightly.

"You may tell her I recommended you to her."

"Not . . . her to me?"

"No. It will hinge on whether or not she wants to live here."

"Is this entrapment?"

"No. She's old enough to be your mother."

And he was old enough to be Felicia's father. Salty studied her soberly. Was she emphasizing such a thing to him?

He said, "Thank you for Mrs. Thompson's name. I do need someone for the boys. I can handle everything else."

"You need not give her cash, although gifts of money on holidays would be acceptable. She only needs a place to live . . . and food. Her pension isn't generous."

"I'll call her."

Felicia added soberly, "If she consents, you will be fortunate."

"Does she drive?"

"Passibly."

"Possibly?" He questioned her pronunciation.

"She can pass the minimum."

"Oh."

"She doesn't do errands. Nor will she chauffeur the boys."

"The boys are reliable. They can handle most situations really very well. I just need someone here as an adult. I can handle the rest."

"See how you take to one another. Have her for tea." Salty smiled.

Softening her thrilling voice, she said to him, "I would bet you can do a tea very well."

"Want to help?" *He'd said that!*

She smiled faintly and lifted her chin just a tad. "I'd be delighted."

Hell. He'd trapped himself! He didn't know how to get out of it. His damned tongue had just blurted the invitation. His body was beyond his control. It wanted her in his house. His subconscious found any way it could to solve getting her.

Salty was stunned. He stared at the magic budding woman and knew she was out of reach for him. Mentally, he knew that it was his body's plotting. His mind needed control. He would get through the meeting with Mrs. Thompson, and he would withdraw his acquaintance with this siren, this lure, this nubile disaster. Yeah. And his soul groaned in despair.

It was just a good thing he'd lived through all the disasters he had, on board ship, beginning with World War II. He knew how to react without betraying his shock.

His mouth said, "I've been an orphan for most of my life. A family is important to me." What he'd said wasn't so bad at face value, but his brain was suspicious. Was he trying to garner her sympathy? He narrowed his eyes as he bit into his busy tongue.

She offered, "My dad still lives. He's in Poland, trying to see if he can influence trade without helping the communists."

"It would be a problem in a country that's under Russia's thumb." Russia also had army advisors in Cuba.

"My father's an optimist. And he's Polish."

"Is he all the family you have?"

"Yes. My mother died in a bombing in France not long after I was born. My dad could never marry any other woman. He really loved my mother."

"Ah." His sound was so compassionate.

She inquired, "What happened to your wife?"

"The boys are adopted. I've never been in one place long enough to be married. I was navy through and through."

She looked skeptical.

"I volunteered for sea duty. I love the sea."

"So you live in Cleveland?"

"We have a boat docked along the lakeshore. It's a good lake. The only difference is the water isn't salty. We go out. The boys can swim like fish."

She grinned. "So can I."

"Well, we'll just see—" But he hadn't stopped his tongue in time.

"All right. I'll hold you to it."

What was he getting into?

He called the boys. They put the dogs on the back screened porch, where the two sat looking soberly out at the departing people as if they were again being abandoned. The boys promised to come back. The dogs weren't convinced.

Salty told Felicia, "Those dogs have to realize they can't be with us all the time."

She looked back at the uncertain dogs with compassion. "Yes."

She had maneuvered her expressive voice into a hollow agreement. He was exasperated. "Come on, get in the car. They'll be perfectly all right."

She got into the car, and Salty felt pleased with her being next to him. He looked over at her, and his look was possessive.

The sooner he got rid of her, the better.

The aunt Felicia lived with came outside and stood around, speaking minimally, viewing Salty with extreme suspicion. She ignored the boys.

Her aunt's car was a rusty brown Nash Rambler wagon that had seen better days.

Felicia volunteered, "The radio is excellent and the clock has never lost a second."

Salty looked at the disaster of the engine and made no reply.

The boys knew cars. They stood on tiptoe and stretched their necks to look into the motor. They discussed what was the matter. They fetched tools and knew which tool was which and how it was used. They were relentless in helping.

Salty explained everything he did. He was patient and clear, and he fixed her car. He replaced the fluids, tested the brakes and spent the entire afternoon getting her car in tip-top shape.

He did that in self-defense. He wanted her car to work so smoothly that she wouldn't have any reason to call on him again. He needed to shun her. He didn't need any excuse to see her again.

When he was finished, the car was back together and running. He said, "You're welcome." And by putting his pointed wolf's teeth into his tongue, he didn't say anything else.

Felicia said, "I'll see you tonight at the theater. Shall I pick you up? My car is running beautifully."

"Thanks," he agreed. Then he hastened to add, "I've got some errands before I go."

"Then you'll be in the play."

He was appalled! When had he decided to do that? He said lamely, "If I do go."

She smiled with such confidence. "You know we need you. This is for a good cause."

"What cause?"

"The children's hospital."

Hell. How was he going to avoid helping with something like that?

Three

Salty met Mrs. Thompson the following Tuesday. He made an English tea, and Felicia came to help. She did the flowers, set the table with a lovely cloth she brought along, and she sampled the goodies.

Salty tapped the back of her hand with a wooden spoon and scolded, "You'll ruin your appetite."

She said something that shivered his nervous system. She said, "I like sampling." And she watched him as she took a cinnamon-sugared grape and closed her soft lips around it.

Salty's heart almost went into cardiac arrest. He chose his words carefully, he spoke minimally, he walked carefully.

Mrs. Thompson brought along her friend, Mrs. Wilder. They looked at Salty critically and without any indication that he wasn't an escaped convict. They looked with jaundiced eyes at the room she'd occupy, and their noses pinched over the gentle dog, Sweetie. Mutt received a cold, dismissive glance.

It was interesting to Salty to see Mutt cheerfully trot out on the back porch and take a nap. He'd been a street dog, so he'd recognized rejection. However, Mutt knew it wasn't a group rejection, it was just that one woman. And it didn't bother the dog.

Mrs. Thompson melted with the food. She became almost animated. She laughed at one of Salty's jokes. And Mrs. Wilder began to be a little competitive for attention.

Generously, Mrs. Thompson called the next day and agreed to move in.

Salty said, "You ought to meet the boys first."

There was no denying that, so Mrs. Thompson came again the next day and met a remarkably slicked-up threesome who were polite and interested. Mutt sat in a doorway and watched. Sweetie lay on a rug by the front door where she could see out easily.

Mrs. Thompson said, "That dog has lost someone dear. Who was it?"

And Salty replied, "Her family had to go to the Far East. The lady, who was left with the dog, was moved to New York. Since there was no one to take Sweetie, the dog went to the animal shelter."

Mrs. Thompson said, "She's grieving."

And Rod agreed, "Yeah."

It was then that Salty decided he could tolerate Mrs. Thompson.

The boys were interested and accepted they'd have another person in the house. It didn't occur to them she might have any real restraint on them. Salty and the three boys had been brought together, so even for another person to be older, another like them wasn't any big deal.

Mrs. T. moved into her room, and the boys were available to run up and down the stairs, carrying and finding and helping.

Mrs. Thompson appeared to accept that as her due. She was gracious to them all. She went into her room and closed the door.

Since Mrs. Thompson had been recommended by her, Felicia was also there helping the new resident to be settled. Then Felicia stayed for supper. She knew what to say to the boys so that they talked, and she reminded them to eat.

After that, Mrs. Thompson appeared for her meals. She exchanged comments on the news. She was very little trouble. She was in the house if there was an emergency, and Salty could leave the boys at home when he went to the play rehearsals. They all settled in. Once, Mrs. Thompson patted Sweetie on the head.

Then Salty brought a female acquaintance home for dinner. Mrs. Thompson brought her knitting down and relentlessly chaperoned the entire evening. She was cold and disapproving and cast censorious eyes on the woman, who was very nice but far too sensitive. Mrs. Thompson froze her out.

Mrs. Thompson's conduct was so different that it caught Salty's attention. Mrs. T. wasn't that way around Felicia. She paid no attention to Felicia's visits. When Felicia was there, the old lady thought nothing of going to her room and closing her door.

Salty was riveted by that thought. Then he wilted. Mrs. T. figured Salty wouldn't be drawn to such a young woman. She thought Felicia was safe with a man as old as Salty. How dispiriting.

At rehearsal the next night, Salty told Felicia, "I had a guest for dinner, and Mrs. Thompson sat like one of the harpies at the guillotine, knitting and casting censorious stares the whole evening. I thought you said that woman wasn't going to be any burden at all."

"Who was she?"

"Who was who?"

"Whom. Who was the woman you brought home?"

"'Whom' is a nice woman who has been very kind to me."

"How kind?"

Salty looked at Felicia in some shock. She was interested in him? If she wasn't, why would she be curious about another woman? Another woman? One other than this she-cat. He didn't dare to ask. What if she said, what if she would be...jealous? What would he do then? His breathing altered. His body tensed. He had to avoid seeing this witch.

So the day after that, Salty said to the boys, "Get all your chores up to snuff, and we'll go out on the boat tomorrow."

When they arrived the next morning at the dock, why was he surprised to see Felicia there in boating whites with good boating shoes? The boys had told her? What was he to do? How could he say to her in front of the boys, "You can't go along because I don't dare spend a day with you!"? How could he do that in front of those three susceptible boys? Hell. He couldn't tell her that if he'd been by himself.

By himself on the boat with Felicia? His imagination went into an overdrive of runaway slide projection of XXX-rated images.

As the boys greeted her exuberantly, Salty's libido was thrillingly filled with the idea of sailing with her...alone.

His stare on her was intense as the wild winds tore off her clothing. Then the mental pictures slowed. He would already be naked. She would look at him and her lips would part. Fires would blaze higher in his sex and he could see the reflection of those in her eyes. She wanted him...now. She—

"Dad, you haven't told Felicia if she can come along. She says she has to have your permission to board."

The boys were so amused.

Felicia watched Salty seriously.

With some fine irony, he said, "Mrs. Thompson isn't along."

"The boys will do fine."

So she realized he was talking chaperons. And she considered herself old enough to need one. She considered that he might—get out of hand? What if he called a cab...and sent the boys home? Would she still go with him, out onto the lake, away from everyone else and spend the whole day with him? Two weeks? Alone, drifting on the gentle swells that mimicked the motions of their bed?

So he realized he wasn't afraid of her lure. He was afraid for his own safety? He suspected she'd chosen to tempt him? She was too young.

That was the trouble. She didn't really realize the dynamite she taunted. She was attracted to him and wasn't aware of his attraction to her. She was trying to catch his attention? Some time along the way, young girls did that with a vulnerable teacher, a priest, a relative or some happenstance boy.

Her femininity was wakening, and she knew she attracted attention. She wanted attention from someone she chose. An older man. She was chaos in the making because she didn't know what came after kisses. She was a nubile disaster waiting to happen. Would the ruination be his? He could lose his boys.

He looked at her, seeing her clearly. He girded his excited loins and braced for the perilous day. He could control himself. He had to.

And it was A Day for Salty.

She laughed as the winds teased her long hair and sculpted her clothing against her exceptionally female body. His soul groaned and his libido went berserk.

She teased the boys and fixed the perfect lunch in the small galley. She sent the boys to Salty with nibbles perfectly made.

She made the outing special just by being along. She exclaimed over the sky. A city girl never realizes how wide the sky actually is. And she looked at the clouds and saw things in them, showing the boys. Since their dad was a sailor, the boys knew the names for the types of clouds, but they'd never made sky pictures before then, never imagined forms in the swirled and puffy clouds.

Salty looked at the same clouds and they were all *XXX*-rated. Didn't she see that? Did she actually think that one was an elephant's head?

And in a cove, they swam. There was a rope-and-rung ladder over the side of the boat. The boys could jump off the side in terrible dives, and she squealed and laughed and had to be coaxed. She stood there in her . . . bathing suit and laughed. Her body was perfect. Her suit was another skin. Salty's body reacted to hers. It was fortunate Salty was sitting down.

They came to him, the laughing boys and that mermaid, and they insisted he come into the water. He didn't want to stand up right then. He said, "In a while."

He went below and found a loose pair of long shorts and put those on. Then he went up and jumped from the well-anchored boat.

They played, and he had the chance to touch her. They all dunked him and he sputtered and chased them all. They laughed and shoved water at him and then went up onto the rocky shore and sat, recovering.

The boys gathered the oval, water-smoothed, thin blue stones and gave them to the mermaid.

She lay back. She said, "You guys are exhausting." She said, "Go away! Let me recover." She said, "That's enough, you rotten pirates." They loved it.

Salty listened to all those words and wanted them whispered to him.

The boys were given a limit to explore the shore. They took off with the endless energy of such ages. They stopped to gather more of the mysteriously perfect, smooth, thin, elongated blue stones.

She turned over onto her stomach and lay the stones into a loop, graduating the sizes to the one perfect largest. "They should be a necklace," she said carelessly.

His ears accepted the words and registered them, but his attention was on her eyelashes, spiked by the water, shadowing her eyes. Her brows were perfect. Who would ever think that long hair, tangled and wet, could be such a lure? Her breasts were delineated with subtle lights and shadows between the protection of her upper arms as she leaned on her elbows. His gaze went down her body to her backside. She had such a sassy bottom. And her legs ...

The boys came shouting, "Come look!"

She got up and turned to him. "Come along." She didn't question. She told him what to do.

He watched her walk confidently away from him. Did she know she could do so, and that he would follow?

But she'd told him something else. And he gathered the blue stones and put them into his back pocket and buttoned it.

The boys had found a fish caught in a watered rift along the shore. It was a big fish, and it was searching for a way out.

They all ate fish, but this one was a prisoner. They caught him with some difficulty, carried him over to the lake and let him go free. They watched him swim away with great satisfaction.

Salty said, "It was stupidity that got him into that fix. We're perpetrating his stupidity in allowing him to live."

Were they impressed? The boys laughed, and Felicia replied, "We all need a little stupidity in order to be human."

Was she that smart? Could she tolerate the absurdity of his attraction to her? Would she be kind enough to allow him to vent his lusts and let him leave with his dignity? Or would she make him her slave?

He considered her. He could handle sexual slavery...to her. He was willing to do anything to relieve this terrible obsession. Why her?

He studied her, already knowing she was perfect. He only confirmed that she was. She was.

And he suffered. He was thirty-eight years old, and he had a nineteen-year-old's sexual crush on a budding woman. He wondered if there was anybody he could go to who wouldn't think he was just a dirty old man.

Thirty-eight wasn't that old.

She was exquisite. The way she moved ... and he was suddenly struck by the fact that she didn't touch him. She touched the boys. She could be less careful about not touching him. She stayed a distance from him. She could stand closer. She laughed at the boys and teased them. She could tease him a little. God. How he wished she'd... No. If she did that, he'd fold. He'd become putty. She would be able to do anything with... He wished.

So he was glum and silent. And he considered that with her around, the boys called him Dad when they were serious. She called him Salty. She could call him Lover or My Own or Darling or Sweetheart. She called him Salty.

Rod asked, "You feeling okay, Dad?"

"Yeah." There was no reassurance there.

"Want us to get the boat and row you back?"

He was highly offended. "Naw. Thanks, anyway. I'm not tired."

She came, leaned over and felt his forehead. She studied him. "What's the matter? Is something bothering you?"

She asked that. What would she do if he told her what was bothering him? He said, "I'm okay."

"Is the play too much? Your part isn't that taxing. Are you bored with it?"

Hell. That was all that kept him going. He got to watch her on the stage. He got to stare at her through the license of acting.

She suggested, "I could talk to Joe. Maybe we could enlarge your part."

"Don't do that."

"The boys know something is bothering you. I've noticed it, too."

Well, she was more sensitive than he'd thought. She understood he was under stress. Why couldn't she realize she was the cause . . . and the cure? He licked his lips and his mouth said, "I'll tell you about it sometime."

She lay a compassionate hand on his bare shoulder. Just her touch scalded his flesh as she said, "I knew there was something. I will listen. I'm your friend. Maybe I can help."

She was so earnest. God help a susceptible man from an earnestly helpful neophyte.

He said to her, "Your lure is as old as time."

But she replied seriously, "So's yours."

He wasn't capable of any other conversation. They went back aboard the waiting boat, rinsed and changed into dry clothing. Salty thoughtfully put the handful of blue stones into his drawer.

They sailed back to their harbor and made the boat shipshape. They went back to their houses, and no other real communication was exchanged.

She knew he was susceptible to her. She in turn was aware of him as a man.

That was a very heady, scary knowledge. He had to be careful of her.

The rehearsals for the play went well. The actors learned their lines and began to stand up and walk around where they were supposed to be and do as they would onstage. It was then the one named Harry had to leave the cast. He'd been a character who was unable to read, and his learning to read was important to the plot.

Salty had been the mute. He was only around as an example of someone unable to communicate. Harry was the one on whom the plot turned. He had to learn, realize the meaning of the words to say the line which clued the others to a disaster that would be averted at the last possible minute.

But they rather liked Salty as a mute and hated to give up having him unable to speak. How could he learn? How could he communicate if he couldn't speak or read and write? They would have to revamp the character. That took rewriting by the playwright, and more rehearsals for Salty with Felicia, who was the play's teacher.

Yeah.

And Joe worked in an attraction between them. Then a kiss.

On being told about it, Salty waylaid Joe and said, "I don't believe the audience will accept a love affair between my character and Felicia's."

Joe shrugged. "The men will understand, and the women will love it."

"I'm too old for her."

"You have a mental block. She's a susceptible female. You're a susceptible male. You two would cause a theatrical explosion. Everyone will come the second night to see this cosmic collision."

"You're using me."

Joe smiled. "Yep."

"And her. You're putting her in jeopardy. I'm not made of clay. I'm a man."

Joe nodded. "Anybody, seeing you, knows that."

"What I'm trying to tell you is that I'm attracted to her already. I don't dare to kiss her."

"You can't live your life trying to avoid reality. So she turns you on. That's great! It'll show in all the movements, in all the sparings as you move about on the stage and wait to kiss her."

"You're a rat." Salty was deadly.

Joe countered, "I'm a brilliant director. I know what's theater. And you, my dear boy, are meat for the grinder of this production. Just do it. Give it life. Live it for the moment. Blow their minds. Upset their libidos. Let them feel your passion."

Salty said a very salty word.

Joe smiled. "You'll survive."

"I'm not sure. I've never felt this way about a woman. She's too young. This could give her grief."

"She's tougher than you think. Felicia has had an interesting life. She wasn't brought up in any convent, you know. She was in Europe, born in France during the war. Her mother and father weren't married.... Ah, you didn't know that. He was in the rabble that tried to flee after the Polish army was gobbled up by Hitler, and he got to France but couldn't get out of the country.

"Everyone was trying to get to America. Her father joined the underground. He stayed there to fight the Germans. His love affair with her mother would make a great film. It had all the heart-tugging nuances. They planned to marry, but Felicia's mother was killed. Felicia has been shifted from pillar to post. All the clichés. She's tough. She comes from stalwart people. Good genes. She can handle being kissed by you on the stage."

"I don't think *I* can handle doing it."

Joe studied Salty. "You're old enough that you can control yourself. You don't need to worry about appearing aroused. Every man in the audience—plus every woman—will be touched by the scene. It will stir their embers."

Hoarsely, Salty asked, "What about mine?"

"It would be remarkable theater."

Almost helplessly, Salty pleaded, "Joe. I could love her."

"My dear boy, you already do."

"My God. Surely not."

Joe swept his whole arm out around him and said, "We all know. We've known all along. If we know, why don't you know such an obvious fact?"

Salty leaned his head back, shut his eyes and took a careful breath. "I've closed it out of my consciousness. It's impossible. She's too young."

Joe guessed, "You've said nothing to her."

"Especially not to her."

"Then it isn't just sex."

"No."

"Hell. I thought it would be simple. This does complicate it. I wonder if Phil could take your role. He wouldn't mind."

"Not Phil." Salty was emphatic.

"Have you someone you can suggest? We're getting too close to deadline."

"Let me think. And, Joe, bend your mind to this. It's a real problem for me."

"I never anticipated this complication."

"I've avoided considering that it is one."

Joe repeated the words, "Is—one."

"Yeah."

By then, their dog Sweetie had become more alert. Her grief was abating with the distraction of the boys' activities. Then, too, Mrs. Thompson was a companion of sorts. Sweetie would follow her around the house and lie beside her chair, and the dog would accompany her outside as the woman inspected the yard and made notes of what Salty was supposed to do.

One day, Salty watched as Mrs. T. carefully went out the front door, down the porch steps and got into a friend's car to go to a movie. The boys were at the

Blakes', and Felicia came in the back door of Salty's almost empty house.

He didn't mention to her that he was alone there. He listened with a feeling of great excitement as the car holding Mrs. T. drove away.

Salty growled to Felicia, "I thought you said the woman would only call the doctor or the police. Do you know that every single day there is a list at my place at the breakfast table telling me what to do that day?"

"It's good for you to have some direction."

Salty studied her sassiness. Then he studied his response to her. He told her in his raspy voice, "Felicia, we have a problem."

"Who?"

"Me and you. Mostly me. We're supposed to kiss in the play."

"Yes. Joe told me."

"Do you mind?"

She bubbled laughter.

"What's that mean?"

"Why should I mind?"

"You go around—just kissing anybody that comes along?"

"I'm eighteen." She was patient and worldly.

"So I can assume that you've gone all the way with anybody who catches your fancy?" His rasp was harsh, his body tense and indignant.

"Kissing and having sex are not synonymous." She was comfortable with the exchange.

He was a little hyper. "So it won't upset you if we kiss on the stage in front of an audience?"

"It's part of the story." She was maturely reasonable.

He was not. "I can't kiss you for the first time on the stage." He drew in a ragged breath. He'd said it aloud.

She smiled just the faintest little bit, but he did have all her attention. She ventured, "You're shy." It was a guess.

It was an out. "Yeah."

"It's just a play." She soothed. "There's no meaning to it. We can practice."

He felt like a heavy, slow-flying bumblebee hovering over a pot of honey. "Yeah," was all his throat managed in the flood of accepting words to reply to such an offer. He added, "It's been a while since I kissed a woman."

"It's still the same old way. Here, let me show you."

And without any further debate or prolongings, she simply came to him, put her sweet, soft body against him, her arms loosely around his shoulders . . . and she lifted that mouth up to his.

It should have been all right, but his arms went around her, his breath was harsh in his nose, he trembled and the sounds were bull-like as he curled his body to hers and took over.

The kiss was incredible. How they managed to stay on their feet was a miracle. Their bodies strained together and their mouths fed on each other, glued as they were. Their brains melted. Their sexes were inflamed and they were stunned.

When he finally realized he must release her or face the consequences of such desire, she was limp. Her face was pale, her eyes almost closed, her lips were swollen and reddened. She looked like a ravaged nymphet.

He was a shambles. His breaths were harsh, he trembled, his muscles had turned to iron, his stare on her was avid.

She had responded. She was as wrecked as he. Thank God they hadn't been onstage for that first kiss. He would have put her over his shoulder and gone off the stage, leaving the audience to entertain themselves.

The problem was, he realized, could they immunize each other so that they could actually kiss one another—onstage—with only reasonable reactions? What if they couldn't?

Again, he rasped, "It's been a while since I kissed a woman."

She formed the words carefully, "You're a danger to the female race. You need to carry a sign or a signal or some sort of warning."

She thought he was dangerous? He was appalled—for a whole minute. Then he began to smile, and his body shivered in a sexual heat. She was susceptible to him? To his kisses? To his thirty-eight-year-old body?

He said craftily, with a thickened rasp, "We'd better do it again. That first time could just've been anticipation. A fluke."

She was forming the word no at the very time he pulled her against him, so her mouth was just right for his invasion. He braced the back of her head against his mouth's pressure as he kissed her without any restraint.

It was all deliberate. He might never get another opportunity, so he did as he'd dreamed all those idle times when he'd thought that all he needed was to kiss her. He'd been so sure he'd be disappointed that he had never anticipated she would react to him in such a way.

He moved his hands on her. He didn't actually molest her, but he came close. He rubbed his body against hers and groaned and extended the kiss to cover the fact that he was taking advantage of her.

His breaths were ragged and his restraint made him shudder as if withstanding a terrible chill.

When he lifted his mouth to suck in oxygen, she said carefully, "You're shivering. Are you shivering?"

And his rasp responded, "Yeah. You're freezing me out. How can I heat you up a little?"

She slitted her big eyes enough to observe him. "If you're chilling, why are you sweating?"

"I need you."

"Bosh."

"I want you."

Was she alarmed for herself? No. Was she compassionate for him? No. She smiled the sly smile of a woman who has a man right where she wants him.

Four

Salty scooped Felicia up across his arms and walked around a little. He was trying to reorient his sense of direction.

She lay lax, curled against him, still stunned, but she managed to say, "Where are you taking me." It was not a real question. Her words were slow and carefully formed.

He explained, "I want to hold you on my lap."

"We wouldn't do that on the stage. We only kiss."

"I did the kiss for the stage practice. Holding you on my lap is for me."

"I'm not your child." She was sure.

"Thank God."

"Why are you thanking God?"

"I wouldn't like you being kin to me. I would really be in a bind."

"You have salacious thoughts about me."

She'd had the cheek to ask that? How was he to reply? "Well—"

"You don't kiss casual."

She gave him that information. HIM! He replied carefully, "I didn't know there were different kinds of kisses." He waited.

She began to smile. He'd hit her humor. After those kisses, he could claim he didn't know there were—differences in kisses? "You're a sly man."

"No. That's my problem." He sat on an easy chair and rearranged her to his satisfaction. Then he kissed her again.

It was better—no, worse. There was no distraction. He didn't have to keep them vertical and on their feet. He could relax and feel sensation all through his body without trying to solve any equilibrium problems. He was hoarse. With his rasp, anyway, he was additionally hoarse. He could barely enunciate coherent words.

She said, "Oh, my—"

His words grated, "What's that mean?"

"I have never been kissed that way in all my life."

She tried to pretend she was knowledgeable? At eighteen? He asked, "How many men have you had?" And he braced for her reply.

"None."

"None?" He gasped in disbelief. And a primal thrill ran through his poor, battered senses. "Oh, Felicia . . ."

"Why are you surprised? What sort of women have you been around? Although this *is* 1962, women are still chattel. We have to save ourselves for the man. We are the helpmate. We are supportive and look nice for a husband. Look at Jackie Kennedy, with her bouffant hair, pillbox hats, wrist gloves and slippers. She's—"

"You're a 'new' woman? Who's been talking to you?"

"My aunts. One really is an aunt, and the others are adopted."

He was suspicious. "Mrs. Thompson?"

"Why do you ask that?"

"She was relentless, chaperoning me that one night."

"She probably guessed you can kiss the way you kissed me just now."

"You liked it?"

"No."

He was stunned. He drew in a breath of anguish.

"You're much too skilled. When women are trying to keep their honor, men like you come along and scramble their brains until they're helpless."

"I'm not that good. I kissed you—"

She smiled.

"And you can talk in complete sentences."

"Why am I on your lap?"

"I find I can't stand up and kiss you at the same time. Kissing you takes all my attention."

She smiled that cat smile of hers.

"I want you."

"No."

"You're here in my house. All's I have to do is carry you upstairs. The boys are at the Blakes', Mrs. T. is gone to a movie. You're alone here with me."

"My aunt has a double-barreled shotgun, and she'd come over here and ram it up your nose."

As his mind repositioned the gun, he asked, "She the one that hawk-eyed me when I fixed your car?"

"Yes. She knows men."

"How come she lets you come over here alone?"

"She thinks Mrs. T. is here."

"So. You like playing with fire."

"Are you fire?" She ran her hand over his chest.

"Yes."

And she said softly, "You feel as if you're on fire."

His raspy voice cracked. "God, woman, you don't know what you do to me."

"You have control. I like lying across you and being kissed by you. You won't do anything I don't want. I trust you."

"Don't."

She pulled down her mouth and frowned at him. "Do I have to get up and make you leave me alone? I really would like you to give me another kiss. I need to see if we can do a reasonable kiss onstage."

"You're taunting me."

"No. I'm enjoying you. I like the way you make me feel. I don't see why you have to get all hyper and excited."

He flopped back and dropped his hands off the sides of the chair arms. He groaned and moved his head side to side very slowly. He was a marvelous picture of frustration.

She watched him and commented, "You're wonderful onstage. You're a natural actor. You emote. You project—marvelously—to the topmost gal— What's funny about that?"

But he kissed her again and wiped her brain clean. Then he started to reeducate her. He instructed her in kissing. He showed her why if he touched her one place, she could feel it in another.

She was careful. She became very wide-eyed. She said, "I'm beginning to understand all the warnings. Men are very subtle and dangerous. They work magic on a woman until she insists."

A shambles, his voice croaked as he asked softly, "Are you insisting?"

"No." She leaned up, braced her hand on his stomach to help herself pry her body up from his sensual nest, and she was carefully free of him.

He lay back, seemingly inert, watching her avidly.

She said, "You must behave more carefully." She was rearranging her clothing back to where it should be.

"You kissed back."

She shifted her shoulders in a fascinating manner as she resettled various parts and their coverings. "I'll be careful, too."

He said the ringer, "We haven't practiced for the stage."

She looked at him hollowly. "How am I ever going to survive a public kiss with you?"

And his ego healed. He suggested, "We need to be locked in a room for two weeks and have our meals passed in to us as we get used to each other."

She said, "My aunt mentioned men saying something just about like that. Is it in the male book for female seduction?"

"Not that I know. I'm facing reality. We have to kiss onstage. We just tried it and look what happened. We'd be dragged to jail on the charge of public salaciousness."

"It was you," she retorted. "I was perfectly confident that I could handle a casual kiss. You're the one who fired it up into such a catastrophe."

"You thought that was a—catastrophe?" He was appalled.

"Chaos? It wasn't a friendly kiss. How'd my clothes get all tangled up that way?"

"I'm wrecked."

She looked at him. His hair was every which way. His clothes were askew. His lap— He looked as if he'd been thrown around by something. Then she saw his eyes. They were bloodshot and the pupils were enormous. She frowned. "Are you all right?"

"No."

"What's wrong?"

He told her readily enough, "You aren't compassionate."

"So now you're saying this emotional mess is my fault? How like a man to blame a woman for his discomfort!"

He told her, "You kissed me."

"I'll ask Joe to kill the kiss."

"If you do, you'll kill me."

She complained, "I thought you were objecting to kissing me."

"I'm objecting to you quitting when you have me on my ear and I hurt for you."

She told him seriously, "I didn't start this."

"Yes, you did. You were going to show me that kissing is done just like always. How many other men have you ruined this way?"

She took the question seriously and replied openly, "I've never before kissed a man the way we kissed just now. I . . . never wanted to . . . before now."

"And now you want to?" He held his breath and he didn't move.

"You scare me. I'm not ready to—go on—past this. I'm afraid." Her marvelous voice trembled. And she looked at him with those big eyes of hers, and she was deadly serious and a little scared.

How could he forget how young she was?

He asked gently, "Do you want me to leave you alone?"

She had a hard time replying. She looked to the side, she looked down, she looked away, she suffered, but she finally said, "No." It was such a soft word.

It was like a lightning rod right up him. He couldn't reply for some time. He couldn't even move. He stared at her, and he knew. He knew. He said, "I'll be careful."

She looked at him with her wounded eyes. She said, "I need to—"

"What?" He slowly moved his marvelous body erect with all the ease of some lazy cat. He stood equally slowly.

She realized he was being careful not to frighten her. He was pretending that he was in control.

She stepped back and only then realized one of her shoes was missing. She hunted it, looking around, found it and put it on.

He growled, "How can you stand there and put a shoe on your foot without becoming unbalanced, when I've got every nerve and muscle working just to keep me upright?"

"It's an automatic reflex. I've done it so many times, my body doesn't need instructions." She was very earnest.

He smiled at her slowly. He said, "Felicia."

She waited. He didn't say anything else. She still waited. He continued to be silent as he watched her. He had rather incredible eyelashes. The lines around his eyes were pale. He had a sailor's fan of squints along his eyes like cowboys or fishermen have. He didn't have deep frown lines. He wouldn't worry or be angered easily. He controlled his own life. He adjusted. He was doing that now. Would his adjustment with her mean that he would discard her?

She said, "Maybe if we're onstage, we can kiss reasonably because we won't think about it."

"I can't not think about you. You're in my mind all the time."

"I . . . like being there."

"Do you love me?"

"I don't know. I have never felt this way before now."

"What scares you about me?"

"You're potent."

"God, yes."

"No. You're the potency of a grown male. It goes beyond kissing. You want control. I'm not sure I want to give control over to you."

He said softly, "You would control me."

Her big eyes closed down a little in disbelief.

He opened a hand out from him. "You're not in my bed, right now."

And that was true. But she pointed out, "This time."

He opened his mouth to draw in a shocked breath and closed his eyes as he lifted his head back.

She said critically, "You're very susceptible."

"Yeah."

"I probably shouldn't stay here, right now. It wouldn't be kind to either of us. I'll have to think about us, and about kissing you."

He told her earnestly, "I'll be thinking the same things."

"Good. Maybe we can figure out if we can go on together."

He said a screening, "Yeah."

She went to the door and out of it. Mutt escorted her across the yard to her car. Salty wasn't in any condition to be out-of-doors in daylight, so he stood on the porch with his hands in his trouser pockets, and he watched her leave him.

When her car was out of sight, his mind kicked in. He went to his room and took out the blue stones. Then he went to the florist, John Noga, and asked the name of a good jeweler.

"Why do you want a jeweler?"

"I want a stone necklace made for a lady."

"Felicia?"

"Now how did you know about Felicia?"

"I guess all Tremont knows."

"Good gravy."

Salty got the name of a jeweler, and the jeweler was interested, but he gave Salty the name of a woman who made crafted jewelry.

Her name was Olivia. She was charmed by the worn blue stone slivers, and she suggested the most subtle of settings so that the stones would be the focus.

Olivia was a clever craftsperson.

Salty was a wily man.

In the morning, several days after that, Joe came over to Salty's house with Felicia. Joe said, "I've been thinking about this kiss business in the play. Your character wouldn't have been with many women. He's shy and self-conscious. He thinks she's a goddess and he's not worthy of her. Being the way he was, he would give a shy, self-conscious kiss to the woman. Without touching her body. It could be very poignant and touching for the audience. An almost worshipful kiss. Women would love it. Men would understand the feeling very well."

Relief ran through Salty like a soothing balm. He replied, "That sounds okay."

"Felicia put some good thought into this and it's her suggestion."

Salty looked at his problem woman. His nemesis. His lure. He said in an ordinary rasp, "That was good theater, figuring that out."

The force of Salty's eyes caused an intimate burning. Couldn't they even just *look* at each other? Why did every word or glance or touch act as if they'd been torched! How was this madness to be controlled?

Joe said, "I've got to see about a dress for Marilyn. She's unhappy that she isn't being dressed with the same care as Felicia. She doesn't realize that it's Felicia's body that makes any rag look as if it was made by a couturier an—"

Felicia interrupted and corrected, "Couturiere."

Joe was kind enough to repeat, "Couturiere. So we must find Marilyn something that makes her feel like Felicia looks. And she won't take Phyllis' advice. God. Being a director is too involved. All's I'm supposed to do is direct the actors in the parts, right? Right. Goodbye."

He left.

Joe had walked right off and left Felicia there, alone, with Salty. With Salty, the boys, the dogs and Mrs. Thompson upstairs in her room. Salty looked at Felicia and tried to hide the hunger in his eyes.

She said busily, "I've come for lunch. I want us to realize that we can be together without tangling and getting all hot and bothered."

He rasped, "I'm already hot and bothered. I've been that way since I first saw you on the stage. That's why I resisted being in the play."

"You took your jacket and shirt off. You could have refused."

"I wanted you to see me naked."

"You kept your pants on."

"Yeah."

She tilted back her head and said in a controlling manner, "You didn't take off your shoes and socks. You didn't remove your trousers or underwear and you didn't chase me around the stage naked. That shows restraint."

"You're walking on the razor's edge."

"No. We're going to be normal people and show that we can sustain a social intercourse without it becoming the other kind."

He warned her with a gruff rasp, "If you play around with words that way, you'll be in trouble."

"No. You have good control and so have I. We'll do all right. We'll be careful." She looked at him as if she could control him and had no doubt that she could.

"A man is a chancy beast."

She scoffed, "If that's so, how can the world be so structured?"

"Beasts get together and get things organized so there is—or isn't—war, depending on their plan. They run things the way they want to."

She countered, "There are men who care about the world, the people and the environment."

"If it works his way."

She considered what had been said; then she commented soberly, "The trouble is, I believe you're right. But it doesn't mean you and I can't get through this intense attraction and survive."

So she admitted it wasn't all his problem. "You want to get rid of me?"

"I don't know. I do want to figure out this fascination. There is something in you that I find so dangerous that it could be fatal for me."

"I'd keep you alive."

She guessed soberly, "With one ankle tied to a tree?"

"Well." His eyes smiled with the danger they'd discussed. "You would rather be tied to a tree than staked out in the sun, wouldn't you?"

"You're a very basic man."

"You're a very nubile, entrancing mantrap. You scare me spitless."

With real curiosity, she asked, "Why?"

"Because you could distance me from living my own life my way. You could get control of me."

"I don't want control of you. I only want to know you."

His attention was riveted on her. "Let's go to bed and get started."

"To you, knowing me is bedding me?"

"It's a distraction to be solved so that I can see beyond it."

"Ah..."

"You understand?"

She sought the right words. "I believe I actually do. You're scary. To go with you would be a whole lot like venturing into dark and unknown lands. Places I don't know. There would be danger."

"That says it pretty well. I'd take care of you."

"You know the risks?"

"Living has always been that way for any man."

"How do you all survive?"

"A lot don't," he admitted. "For the rest, we try to choose sides well enough to make living reasonable enough and protect the ones that are our responsibility."

She observed slowly, "You make the simple act of living into a different thing than I've ever thought about. Life isn't easy, is it." It was not a question.

"Your parents knew. They took what they could and helped where and how they could. They had you."

She was surprised. "How do you know it was so?"

"Joe."

"He told you about my parents?"

Salty replied, "Some. Enough. They were good people, and you're something they'd be proud about."

She was somewhat wistful, "I wish I could have known my mother."

"She's in you. You're the same kind of people she was. She and your father would claim you as theirs with some pride."

She turned her head to look out of the window. Then she looked at him as she said, "I've never thought of the world as being as you've described. But when I think about it, you've said it right. All the varying levels of struggles for power are male strivings. Violent struggles or political struggles and the combination. It's all there. We just don't realize it's exactly what you've said. Men making places for themselves, one way or another, at one level or another."

He asked gently, "How has it been for you? You had only your hawk-eyed aunt."

"As men gather other men, women gather women— but as friends, not as a pack to run with. I've been lucky in those who have cared for me."

"Does your hawk-eyed aunt belong to your mother or your father?"

"My mother," she replied. "My father's people are lost to me. We don't know where mother's family has gone. All was chaos. All contacts were lost."

"All wars are that way," he responded kindly. Then he added gently, "We had to stop Hitler."

She said sadly, "We are sending men to Vietnam."

"Yeah, Eisenhower sent advisors and that was foolish. Kennedy is stepping it up. God knows why. The French had tangled for control over the natives for seventeen years and made no change. We are stupid to get involved. Those people are determined to run their own country."

She asked, "Is it the Chinese?"

"Vietnam isn't Korea."

"How do you know?"

He told her, "I've been all over the world. I've talked to guys and listened and read. If you spread your resources, you get more answers, and you're better able to judge."

She considered him. "I believe I could kiss you now and keep control."

"I don't think I could. All this talk about men and competition has my testosterone shivering and ready."

"You mean it isn't me, it's challenge that sets you off?"

"I want you."

"Why did you have that woman over here when Mrs. T. had to chaperon?"

He frowned at the nubile witch. "She was a nice woman. Mrs. T. scared her off for good."

"I don't believe you've answered my question. Why did you have her here?"

He was surprised. "I did answer. She was a nice woman who came to dinner."

"Were you trying to get her into bed?"

"By golly, I wish I'd thought of that! She might have been willing!"

"You beast!"

And he laughed.

How like a man to taunt a woman and then laugh at her indignation.

She said, "I have to go. Goodbye."

His arm snaked out and his hand clasped onto her arm like a vise. It was the first time he'd touched her in days, and they were both riveted.

She twisted her body a little and frowned. "You're holding on too tightly."

His lips parted and he looked down at his grasp in surprise. "Sorry." He released her and rubbed the whitened flesh. "I was afraid you'd get away. You promised to stay for lunch."

"I don't think—"

"Felicia! You're here!" There were three jubilant versions of that exclamation. The boys tumbled inside with the two dogs who pranced and were equally jubilant, but they didn't bark. Mrs. T. forbade dogs to bark in the house.

Felicia smiled down at the boys. She was glad to see them. She listened to their greetings and smiled and smiled and smiled and smiled. She touched each one as they spoke. She smoothed hair or touched a shoulder or cheek. She liked them.

She even spoke quietly to the two dogs, who wanted their share of her attentions.

Salty noted it all and was sulky. Why couldn't she be just as glad to see him? All she did was scold him. She didn't give him any of those fond glances or gentle

laughter. She didn't voluntarily touch him. She...
resisted him.

The boys went thundering up the stairs, quietened by
the thick, padded stair carpet that Mrs. T. had insisted
on, and the dogs went willingly back outside. They had
become accustomed to living there and had adjusted to
the new rules.

As Felicia closed the door after the dogs, Salty
growled in his rasp, "I ought to be a dog who dances on
his front paws while he wags his tail and lolls out his
tongue, smiling at you, then maybe you'd pay attention
to me."

She smiled just a bit. "Let's see if you can do something like that."

He came to her, took her rather roughly into his arms
and he did support the back of her head as he kissed her.

It was thrilling. The same churning disorientation.
The same hot response. All the same.

He lifted his mouth from hers and looked at her soberly.

She managed to move her lips, and he watched her
mouth as if he'd never seen anything like moving lips.
She said, "I thought we were going to be more careful."

Only then did he realize that his iron muscles were all
that was keeping her from sliding to the floor. He had
the gall to question, "I do that to you?" But he smiled
like a Cheshire cat.

"You beast."

"I've been telling you that this whole time. It took
some convincing. How cowardly are you? Wait. I know
you're cowardly or you wouldn't run off all the time.
What I need to know is, how brave are you?"

Hanging in his arms, incapable of standing firmly on her feet, she replied, "I'm my own woman."

If he hadn't already loved her, she would have caught him then. He smiled down at her and knew the truth. He did love her. It was the worst kind of love, for it could be forever. Past death. Into other lives. Throughout time.

She was too young.

She said, "Help me stand up so I can help with the table. With the kids all around and the dogs and Mrs. T., I should be safe enough from you. Let me go."

He said, "You're mush. You can't even stand up. You need some injections to make you stronger."

"I take vitamins."

"My injections."

She didn't know what he was talking about and righted herself by holding on to his shoulder and putting her hand to her head to reorient herself. She asked quietly, "What time is it?"

"What time?"

She was more specific. "Which meal?"

He looked at her face. She was serious. He could have that much influence on her senses? Did she realize how much she loved him? He was going to get her.

Five

When Salty and Felicia practiced that night on the stage, the scene was carefully directed. Joe suggested stage movements as the two built the audience up to the kiss. They practiced the moving about and the calculated tension.

Joe watched and corrected or changed or suggested, and the two puppets were maneuvered around for the most impact on those watching. At first, the two didn't kiss. When they came to the kiss, they stopped and looked at each other. Almost immediately, they broke eye contact and moved aside.

Their bodies were aware of the deliberate suspense. That had been carefully built by Joe's manipulation of their movements from the time they first met at the beginning of Act I.

Until the kiss was added and the deliberately calculated buildup of tension, Salty hadn't realized the finesse of a good director. In the navy, they'd done plays. The directors mostly kept track of things, told the actors what to do, and they did it. But for some reason, none of the plays they'd done had the subtle nuances of building sexual intensity. Not on board ship.

With the gradual change in Salty's character, a different slant was put on the original play. Because one man had had to leave, and the volunteer understudy had fallen down a stairwell and was in traction, it had been too late to work in another actor for that pivotal role. The adjustment of the playwright, in who would do what, had created a subtle variation that now added explosive sensual suspense to the cliff-hanging danger.

Poor Salty.

Salty said to Joe, "If you're a sadist, your expertise should be sold to the Russians. I'm not sure I'll be able to handle this."

A work-overloaded Joe gestured in impatient hand circles as he said variations of, "Find an outlet, take care of yourself, talk to a eunuch, don't bother me, I have my own problems and your whining is one."

He offended Salty. Sailors did not whine.

But they could suffer.

With the devastation of the practice kiss at his house, Salty was riding on the edge of desperation with Felicia.

He called Linda Sawyer, the pliant woman whom Mrs. T. had intimidated. He invited Linda to dinner. He washed his car and vacuumed it meticulously. He got a haircut, shaved with exquisite care, spruced himself up and went to pick her up.

Linda was delighted to see him again, "Salty!"

He grinned. "I hope you don't mind going out to eat. Mrs. Thompson couldn't come along." And he laughed.

"I was afraid that old harpy had you under her witch's spell!"

"She had no taste at all." He smiled like a ruttish goat.

"It's wonderful you were able to sneak out tonight. How I've missed seeing you!" And she voluntarily threw her arms around him, pressing her soft body to his, and she kissed him!

He found he was a little shocked. That surprised him immeasurably. When had any woman shocked him before then? That was unusual. Well. He'd been taking care of a teenager, an old lady and small children. He was out of practice. He could handle a willing woman.

The couple went out to a very fine restaurant. Salty consulted with her over the food and made suggestions. They discussed foods that were perfect.

He ordered for her. Then he toasted her with his wine.

Linda was faintly flushed and wiggly and animated. Her laugh was intimate and good. Her eyes sparkled. She touched his arm.

He smiled and was charming. He listened to what she said with avid attention. He encouraged her to talk, and he admired her.

As the evening progressed, he realized that Linda was a jewel of a woman. She was funny, she was discreet, she was charming, she was gentle and she liked him. She flirted.

And he faced the fact that he couldn't go to bed with her... only because... she wasn't Felicia.

That was a stunning revelation for a career sailor who, at thirty-eight, was still single.

Now, how was he to get out of this situation? He couldn't hurt Linda's feelings and just dump her. He couldn't take her home and abandon her. He was going to have to do something.

He blurted earnestly, "I have a friend I want you to meet. He's one of the best friends I have, and he's a good man. I asked you here tonight because I wanted to be sure you're available."

After his first sentence, her face became still, her movements stopped, her animation disappeared. "I thought—"

Salty barreled along, "He's a little shy. You'll have to work on him to get him comfortable. I don't know of any woman who is more compassionate with a male ego than you." He looked at her bleakly and went on, "You'd be perfect for any man."

She was very sober. He'd shocked her. Her face became pale and serious. She said softly, "I'll see."

"Let me bring him over to meet you."

Linda didn't reply right away; then she said, "Not right away. Maybe later."

"So you're busy right now?"

"Not especially." She lifted her chin and looked straight at him. "I've had a—disappointment."

"Anything I can help with?"

"Not anymore."

There was a long silence. Then he began to tell her tales about the navy and himself, and he disparaged himself the entire time. He was clumsy and stupid.

She wasn't fooled. If anything, it only underlined the kind of man he was. He was trying to appear useless to her. Unattractive. It only proved how kind he was.

He took Linda home too early, and he spoke again of his friend. He didn't give the friend a name because he hadn't had the opportunity to pick out the sterling character for review. She was noncommittal.

At her door, she asked for a goodbye kiss. That was her word. Goodbye. Not good-night, but goodbye. He held her gently, and his kiss was kind and gentle. She returned it with equal gentleness. She didn't try to seduce him. It was all very poignant.

Salty went back to his car and got in the driver's seat to sit there with a great sigh of despair. Felicia was too young. It was going to take a while to get over her, to get past this fascination of a nubile witch less than half his age.

He returned to his own house in glum resignation, moving like a defeated man.

Who should be there but Felicia! She was reading to his sons. Did she greet him with exuberance? No. She knew. She sat there sober faced, her big eyes even bigger, and she studied him with deadly dire but silent accusation.

He felt he was guilty and that made him restless and a little hostile. He greeted the boys, patted the dogs and exchanged neutral nods with Mrs. T. Then he looked on Felicia who, with slow dismissal, then went back to the book she was reading. She was mad at him.

He said pleasantly, "What are you doing here tonight, Felicia?"

She moved her head up to indifferently view the talking stranger and replied, "How was it?"

Since she was that hostile, his libido expanded as he replied, "Great."

No one said anything. The boys were unaware, Mrs. T. sat by the invisible guillotine, still knitting. The dogs returned to their cedar bags to curl down and watch, bite at something in their fur and lick. Felicia indifferently went back to the book and began to read, so the boys went back to crowd around her and listen and watch the words.

Abandoned in the middle of his own—rented—living room, Salty considered all the things he could say or do and, having abandoned a good woman and now been abandoned himself, he abandoned them all. He went up the stairs and changed into jeans. Then he went downstairs to edge his way back into Felicia's life, but she was gone.

She'd vanished. The nasty little underage feline witch had gotten up and left while he was upstairs. There is nothing more aggravating than a woman who doesn't know to sit still until a man can get around to reasserting himself.

In the summer days that followed, Salty planted all sorts of fall flowers in his rented yard. Mrs. T. directed him. The boys were underfoot and very willing help.

He took the boys sailing and wore them out so that he could sleep.

No such luck.

He prowled at night. He prowled inside until Mrs. T. inquired nastily, "What are you doing, up all night? Why don't you be quiet and let a body sleep?"

So he prowled outside. The police stopped him once and weren't patient. He had to prove who he was, and he got really irritated and dangerously polite. The police loved it and pushed verbally. Salty was willing to counter until they laughed at him.

After that, they waved as they went around the area.

So he became a little lean and mean. He'd sit in the yard swing with young kids all over him and dogs barking. He was there, but he wasn't with them at all.

His body went through the movements, and his tongue said the cautionings and rules without his full attention. But he did notice that Sweetie was again a vigorous animal. She was frisky for a nine-year-old, and she loved the kids. She loved him, too, and would stand, waiting for his attention. He gave it automatically. She wasn't critical or repulsed. She understood grieving.

"Why isn't Felicia ever here?" Salty got really tired of hearing that. He'd shrug, but he wouldn't reply.

And at rehearsals, his stalking of Felicia became a sexual dance that was so intense the others would watch in wordless fascination. When practice broke up, he could hear "It exhausts me to watch them," and the re-plying variations of "'Exhaustion' isn't the right word." And there'd be empathetic, soft male laughter.

Salty looked at other women. He met a couple for lunches. They were all perfect. But they weren't Felicia.

Salty recalled the time-travel film with Joseph Cotten in which Jennifer Jones came back to him at different ages until she finally came to him, old enough.

So he'd daydream of Felicia coming to him, thirty years old. But instead of being relieved that she was closer to his age, he'd question her closely about other men.

In his imaginings, she'd ask, "And...at thirty-eight...you're whatever is the male version of a vir-gin?" He'd be indignant. That was just about exactly what that siren would say.

And he'd ask God just what His purpose was in throwing two such unsuitable people together this way? But that only made him realize he hadn't seen Felicia outside the theater.

She was avoiding him.

How like a woman to get huffy and snub a good man just because he had an innocent dinner with a friend.

Suppose Felicia was having...dinner with a...friend?

He became hyper. He started out of the house and was almost across the yard when he realized he hadn't shaved. He was dirty from digging dandelions under the pointing finger of the old harpy sheltered in his house.

He went back inside, showered, shaved and put on fresh clothing. He wore slacks, a shirt with the cuffs turned up twice and loafers. He combed his hair.

As he crossed the living room, the boys asked, "Can we go?"

He replied, "No." And he went on out of the house, down the alley and over to the witch's house.

The hawk-eyed aunt was there. Salty asked, "Is Felicia here?"

She replied, "No."

"Who's she seeing?"

"Not you."

"I've noticed. Where is she?"

"If she wants to see you, she'll do so."

Salty surveyed the hawk-eyed woman and knew she was attractive and probably three years younger than he. How did she feel about an older man coming there in the middle of the day and asking for her niece? It probably irritated her.

He said abruptly, "You're not married?"

She slapped the word down like a card on a table. "No."

"You probably ought to be married." He turned away and walked back home.

The hawk-eyed one turned her head and looked up at a second-floor window. Felicia lifted back the curtain, and the two exchanged an unsmiling look of communication. Then Felicia dropped the curtain, and her aunt went back into the house.

Back at his own house, Salty phoned Felicia, but she was never there. The hawk-eyed one said that. At rehearsal, Salty asked Felicia, "Where were you all day?"

She snubbed him. "At home."

"Why'd your hawk-eyed aunt say you weren't there?"

"I told her to."

"Why?"

"Are you that stupid?"

It gave him something to chew on. But he couldn't think of any reason for her to be that *p-p-peeved* with him. Because of Mrs. T., Salty was watching his salty language.

At the next rehearsal, Salty was adult about it. He said to Felicia, "Just because we don't agree on things is no reason to stay away from the kids. They miss you." They'd never said anything about missing her, but guilt was good for a woman.

She replied, "I see them just about every day."

He was shocked. "When?"

And she enunciated the words, "When you're not there."

Restless, impatient, he sought something, anything to distract him from Felicia. He began to look for a man for his rejected friend Linda.

He hit on the miracle idea of asking Felicia's help! Women like to matchmake. They were interested in a woman getting some reluctant man. They loved plotting. He'd get her involved with finding a man for Linda. Simple. Crafty. Perfect.

Since she wouldn't take phone calls from him, he had to wait for rehearsals to ask Felicia, "Do you know any men around thirty who are shy and easy with a woman?''

And what did she do? She nailed him with a killing look and replied, "That's too old for me."

He considered turning her over his knee and giving that sassy, unpliant pre-woman a taste of what she'd obviously missed in growing up. She had no respect for adults—and she had told him that even thirty was too old for her. Therefore she was telling him, loud and clear, that thirty-eight was past all limits. Yeah.

He went around slumped as much as his bulldog build would allow, feeling he was at the end of his life. His thirty-eight-year-old body indicated that he was not. He told it to knock it off. And his body was amused.

Why was it that a man couldn't even control his own processes? His mind went on adventures without his permission; his body hungered for relief. His reactions to others could be beyond his instant control. A man was supposed to be the captain of his ship and the master of his soul.

It didn't always work out that way.

His sneaky, independent mind decided he could kill several birds in the bush by asking the help of ole Hawk Eyes. She'd lived in that area for some time. There were single people. The women went to church, so their acquaintance was wide. She ought to be able to help him find women to add to the male party he was going to have for Linda.

Salty washed and shaved and put on deodorant and clean clothes thinking what a nuisance women are. Instead of driving, he walked over to Hawk Eyes's house to calm himself into appearing civilized. And he considered the logic of pillage and capture in olden times, which made good sense. What a simple solution! Why give females alternatives?

He had enough contacts through the navy personnel who had settled in Cleveland that he could scare up a nice, already trained assault, search and rescue band. He'd get first dibs on directing the first foray.

He stood on the street and considered her house. It would be easy. But he went solitarily up onto the porch and knocked with courtesy.

Predictably, Hawk Eyes came to the door.

He said courteously, "I'd like to discuss something with you. May I come in?"

She studied him coldly. Then she opened the door. He took it from her to go inside, but she came out on the porch, instead. She stood, her arms crossed across her chest, and she looked at him with endurance.

He was older than she, he could be cordial. He said, "I have a problem."

She nodded once, rather more elaborately than need be.

She had agreed that he had a problem. Who'd asked for her opinion? She ticked him. God help the man that ever was drawn to this one. But, no man would get past the bramble-bush barrier of her attitude.

Clinging to his politeness, he said, "I have a woman friend—"

"I know."

He gave Hawk Eyes a stern glance and went on, "Who is about your age. She doesn't know very many people in Cleveland. It would be nice if someone could help her get acquainted. I'm new here, myself, and I don't know very many people. Could you help with—"

"No."

"I can find some men. That's not the problem. But I can't have one woman over to meet a houseful of men. You're the only person I know who is about her age. Would you help me find some women to come to the party?"

"For...you?"

"No. I've recently been cured of women." He spoke firmly, he projected the sound, and he allowed his voice to indicate the futility of trying to attract anyone to himself. He was only out to help a woman find a man.

And Hawk Eyes considered it. She said, "I'll let you know by tomorrow."

He asked, "What is your real name? Felicia never told me." If she should come to his house, he could hardly introduce her by the label he'd given her. As Hawk Eyes hesitated to reveal her name, he pushed. He mentioned, "I can hardly call you Aunt."

She moved her tongue in her closed mouth to count her teeth so that she wouldn't smile.

When she simply waited silently for him to leave, he gave her a card he'd just had printed. It gave his full name, navy rank, address and phone number.

Still silent, she watched him as he said, "I'll wait for your call." She said nothing. He went across the porch, down the steps and the walk home didn't bring his blood pressure down at all. He told the kids he'd be back for supper, and he left.

He went to the dock, took his boat out of there and sailed against a strong wind for two hours as he calmed down, discussed conduct with his guardian, and even called up his dead parents, who had never replied no matter what sort of problem he had.

He decided he'd invite Felicia to attend the party, whether or not old Hawk Eyes capitulated. Maybe Linda

would come up with another woman or two. That made
him sour. Linda would probably find some woman who
was forty years old and "just right" for him.

Well, he was thirty-eight.

Perhaps Linda would find a woman about thirty-five.
If the forty-year-old was *amiable,* he already had three
sons. She wouldn't have to have kids. He was in the
market for a woman. One of his own.

But when he conjured one, it was always Felicia. He
had a bad case of her. He needed distraction. Something beyond just a woman in bed. He hadn't been able
to handle that. Linda had been willing. His body was
loyal to—Felicia. And she wouldn't even speak to him.

So at rehearsal that night, when it came to the kiss, he
took that pre-woman into his arms and he let out all the
stops. He really kissed her. He would have stopped, but
she was kissing back, so he kissed her into shambles. She
was wet noodles in his iron arms. Her face was pale, her
eyes closed, and he shivered.

The cast went berserk. They cheered and clapped and
stomped and were completely out of hand.

He watched his woman. Her lips moved. He had to
bend over her to hear, and the avidly watching Phyllis
fainted. Salty was only peripherally aware of the fuss
Phyllis caused. He was making out Felicia's whisper. She
said, "You are a rat."

His rasp agreed. "I'm a ship's water rat. I live in a
ship's black hold and I have no rules."

She nodded her wobbly head in agreement.

He commanded, "Come to my party. Promise on
your tattered honor."

She nodded in such a wobble that she could have been
refusing.

In a harsh rasp, he said, "You agreed. You're committed."

She formed the words, "Blackmail."

And he said, "Yeah. But you can't wiggle out of this. I'd come to your house and drag you to mine by the hair of your head, with the boys running along and the dogs barking. It isn't something boys and dogs should witness. You'll have to come voluntarily."

She opened her eyes a slit and soberly accepted that was so.

Salty thought he was the one who'd won. Women do stuff like that. Men are hard enough to lead. Sometimes they need to feel they are in control.

With Phyllis ruined for the evening of rehearsal, discipline was broken, and Joe gave up. They all went home. Salty followed Felicia to her house, got out of his car and went to hers to open the door. Then he guided her over to his car and put her into it.

He went around to the driver's side, got in and immediately drove away before she could get organized enough to ask him anything.

Actually, she had asked several times, "Where are we going?"

But he didn't reply. He took her to the dock. He greeted the watchman and said, "We're not going out."

Then he took her on board and down into the cramped cabin. She cautiously sat on the pullout sofa and waited for him to explain himself. He stood with his head bent over in the limited space, and he looked at her, trying to control basics. Trying to think on past them and soothe her enough that she wouldn't panic.

She asked the obvious question, "Why are we here?" He had told the watchman they weren't leaving the dock to sail.

He really didn't know why he had her there, except that he needed her with him. "I want to talk to you."

She was logical in trying to make him admit why they were there. "We could have talked at my house."

Her house? That hawk-eyed aunt's den. He asked quickly, needing the information, "What's your aunt's name?"

Of all things, Felicia hadn't thought her aunt's name was a subject for such a meeting. She asked impatiently, "You don't know?"

"If I knew, I wouldn't have to ask." He recognized a stupid conversation when he heard it. But they had to get past these preliminaries before they could get to anything that made sense.

"Her name's Emilie Strode."

"I needed to know. I couldn't introduce her as Hawk Eyes at my party."

"What party?"

"I'm giving a party to introduce Linda Sawyer to more people."

"Intro— Get out of my way." She started up from the sofa.

He put his hands on her shoulders and kept her in place as he complained, "Somehow I knew you'd react just this way. You're a selfish woman who looks on all other women as competition. You need to be more kind to other people."

That fired her up. "You don't know anything about me, at all."

He retorted, "You telegraph every move from five miles out."

"Baloney."

"Is that the new word for high—" And his tongue stopped.

In deadly calm, she inquired, "For high—what?"

He tried, "High-falutin' women?"

"That isn't the word that stopped you. Was it high *school?*"

"Why would I say that?"

She was sarcastic, "You were being derisive about my age."

"Never." His reply was quick and very earnest.

"Yes. Let me past."

"No. Felicia—"

She stopped struggling in order to be very serious. "The only time you treat me as a woman is when you want to get me into bed."

"No. I've been trying to give you up."

She was shocked. "What!"

"I'm too old for you."

She bubbled laughter.

"I'm twenty years older than you."

She sat back down and tilted her head back. She was sassy. "That almost makes us even. You've probably learned enough so we can be near the same level."

He sat down beside her on the pullout couch. He was just about at his wits' end. He was haggard and his hair was tousled. His evening beard was obvious. He told this big-eyed pre-woman, who was a witch, "I don't know what to do about you."

She was impatient. She sassed, "You're thirty-eight years old and don't know? No wonder you're still not married."

He looked at her. Her hair, too, was untidy from the wind on the lake. She had been buffeted by it as they'd boarded. There in the semidarkness of his boat's cabin, she looked like a tousled wanton. She looked accepting.

She'd said he was old enough to know what to do with a woman.

Did she mean it? His face was so vulnerable. His rasp was rough as he asked her, "Teach me."

Six

Felicia used her remarkable voice as she asked with husky impatience, "Is this what they mean about a woman's work never being done?"

Salty sat next to her and didn't look over his shoulder at her as he replied pithily, "Yeah."

"I'm supposed to teach you to seduce me?"

"You wanna be seduced?" He was shocked and turned his head to stare.

She hesitated for some little time before she said in her lightened *basso profundo* voice, "You could try."

He dismissed that with some bitterness. "You like to see a guy hanging on wires?"

She considered his words. He'd be hanged? She was of the age of consent. "Why would a seduction hang a guy?"

"You'd be coy, but you'd stop me at the last minute. You'd like to see me strung out and hanging, but I'm not even going to try with you. Temporarily satisfying me wouldn't solve my problem with you." He put his head in his hands and his elbows on his knees. "Neither war I was in was this bad."

"What do you mean?" Her low voice trembled as she put her hand softly on his back.

He lifted his head back while still looking at the floor and said, "We can't talk about anything, except that you gotta help me with this party. You got to convince Haw—Emilie that she's got to find some women for my party. Not your age—you're too young for the guys I know." He turned his head and looked at Felicia, who was again all eyes. "You're too young for me, too. I know that."

"Who says?"

He turned away. "I say. I'll get over you, probably. I'll work at it. You're a special woman...well, you'll be one someday, but I won't be around to watch that."

"Where will you be?"

"I don't know. Away."

"There's nothing wrong with Cleveland. This is a good city."

"I can't risk running across you by accident. I have a fatal case of you. I have to protect myself. I'm giving you up."

Her voice changed and was throaty and wicked. "So you're letting me go?"

"I never had you *to* let you go."

Her low voice dragged as she chose words, "Why do you think I'm keeping contact with your boys?"

He dismissed that. "They're nice kids."

"They tell me—everything."

His head swiveled around, and he asked in a raspier rasp, "You really are curious about me?"

"Yes."

"You don't have to ask kids to find out. You oughta come to the source. I can tell you anything you want to know." He shifted on the sofa so that he faced her better. He could have hope? He'd given her up. Almost. He'd been trying to do that.

She lay back against the cushions, and he loomed in front of her.

He was aware of looming. A man with his bulldog build used that to his advantage in many circumstances. Especially on board ship intimidating young recruits. But to become a lover, he didn't want to frighten or intimidate this witch. Not right away. He wanted to appear needy and as frustrated and discouraged as he actually was.

His lashes screened his eyes only because he had to look down at her to judge her feeling of safety. He needed her to feel secure. From him. For now.

She had such big eyes. With her immaturity, her eyes were enormous. She looked very vulnerable and isolated. Naturally, she *was* isolated. That's why he'd brought her out there. He'd had to get her alone, with no chance of anyone intruding on their exchange.

He'd only wanted to talk. He needed help with the party for Linda. He still felt bad that he hadn't been able to respond to Linda. He knew what being rejected did to a person. Linda was too nice not to have some good man.

While Felicia was too young for him, her kisses hadn't ever been casual. And she was susceptible to him. He could whammy her with a kiss. He'd proven it was so, just that very night, on the stage in front of all those cheering people.

But was she just beginning to be a woman and was therefore susceptible to any man? Or was she only interested in him?

He would kiss her again. Soon. In private. Without all those kids and dogs and Mrs. T., or Hawk Eyes around.

Right now, Salty had Felicia trapped there with him. If she'd been smart, she would have told the watchman, "I'm alone with this man. I don't want to be with him!" She was old enough to've known that. She was there—with him—of her own free will, and she had told him right out loud that she was curious about him.

What was there about him that made her curious? Talking? Conduct? Sex? She was the age to be curious and ready to experiment. Was she? Maybe not. She'd been trained by Hawk Ey—Emilie.

It was probably only by Emilie's being old Hawk Eyes that Felicia had been untouched up until then. Felicia's kisses were unfair in the game of getting acquainted. She kissed serious. She had never kissed him casually. It had been flat-out sex the entire time. The upper persuasion to a lower invasion.

His body groaned and tortured him. With her safely there on his boat, with his body blocking her getaway, he asked, "Why are you here with me?"

"You brought me here."

"You could have declined."

"I was never given the opportunity."

She was putting all the weight of conduct on his shoulders. His were broad, he could handle the responsibility. "Do you know what happens to careless little girls that don't pay attention or object?"

"Nothing."

His raspy voice made a disbelieving sound.

She retorted with some confident sass, "I have you to protect me."

Oh, hell. There is nothing more asinine than a female who lays all of her trust on a chancy man. What's he supposed to do then? Either he obeys or he hears about it all the rest of his life.

He asked her, "Will you talk to your aunt about my party?"

"Am I invited?"

And he thought about the reaction of all the guys to her. He'd have to make her wear a pillowcase over her head. "Will you wear a pillowcase over your head?"

"A pillowcase?" She seemed dubious.

His rasp was tender. "I'd cut eyeholes for you."

"How gracious of you."

"I can't have any of the guys thinking you're in the market for another man."

"I've never had a man. How could I have 'another' man?"

His rasp was hoarse. "You could have me first."

She smiled a cat's smile, watching him.

How was a grown man to survive a nubile flirting witch who didn't really know what she was doing? "Do you know what you're doing to me?"

"I'm . . . flirting."

He warned her, "You're playing with fire."

"You're going to . . . burn me?"

Very gravelly, his voice explained, "I'm on fire. I could scorch you pretty bad."

"I'll see if I can handle it." She asked sassily, "Do I use unguent or Vaseline ointment?"

He asked, "Where?"

"On my burns."

"Depends where they are." He leaned over and scooped her from the pillows against his fiery body. He held her against him and groaned as if his very soul was writhing in the flames.

She was caught by the sound. She put her hand to his head, gently finger combing back his hair. "I don't mean to make you suffer. Are you teasing me, or are you really that—that much in pain?"

He squeezed her sweet, soft body impossibly closer and his breaths were like the winds from flames. "I'm being very brave," he groaned against her throat. "If you knew the extent of my suffering, you'd forget everything you've been taught and give me...surcease."

She was young. She asked sassily, "Has this ever worked before now?"

He stilled. Then he began to release her, loosening his greedy hands, relaxing his rigid arms. He lifted his ravaged face and looked at her with bloodshot eyes. He couldn't think of anything to say. He put her aside, stood up and smothered a groan as his body objected to the movement away from her. He put his hands into his trouser pockets and hunched his shoulders. He closed his eyes and suffered.

And she was caught by his ordeal. She was alarmed for him. She also stood up and was compassionately empathetic. She said, "Salty? Are you all right?"

He grated, "I'll live. Probably."

She thought he was teasing and chuckled for his humor.

He didn't laugh or respond. He was still trying for control of the chaos she always built in him.

She wasn't stupid, only young, and she came to understand he was struggling with a power she didn't realize had existed. She said, "Oh, Salty. I am sorry."

"I'll be okay."

"What can I do to help you?"

"Sit down and don't say anything." He moved his head and shifted his stance. And he suffered.

She was silent, watching with concern, compassion.

He said, "This isn't working. I can't forget you're there. Go up on deck. I'll be up in a couple of minutes."

"Salty—"

"Please. Don't. I'm hanging on those wires."

She went quietly past him and up onto the sailboat's deck. The winds were strong and invigorating. She turned her face to them and closed her eyes. She thought of the power of sex and she suffered with the big man who was in its throes.

Her attraction to him was exciting and thrilling, but she didn't suffer from just being near him. Why would it be worse for him? And she remembered a cat they'd had to keep in the house because she was in heat. The cat's pupils had been enormous and her eyes were limpid as she purred and begged to get out of the house, *meowing,* pleading. And she remembered how sympathetic Emilie had been to the cat.

Emilie.

Emilie had taken care of Felicia all of her life. She'd never married. She'd been devoted to caring for Felicia. And Felicia remembered the fragments of a quarrel Emilie had had with a man who'd wanted her to put Felicia up for adoption.

Emilie had wanted the man. Who had he been? Felicia had been young. Five? Seven? Gangly. All eyes. Had the man given Emilie an ultimatum? Had Emilie been figuratively locked in a house when she'd wanted a man?

But she'd been obligated to take care of Felicia. Had Emilie's life been ruined by Felicia?

When Salty came up on deck, it was to a very sobered Felicia. She asked, "Are you all right?"

"Yeah."

"If you have the party—when—you have it—would you include a man for Emilie?"

"Sure."

"You won't mention your name for her to the men?"

"Naw."

"I'll help."

"I'm not sure I want you there."

She stilled. "Oh."

"I don't want another man to see you."

She smiled. "No one else looks at me."

He was stunned. She wasn't looking at other men? She didn't see that men's faces changed when Felicia was there? Around Felicia, men's faces were like those of the men around the film goddess, Marilyn Monroe. Their faces were vulnerable. Soft. Entranced. Felicia didn't see that in the men who watched her? Good.

"Well," he said generously, "wear a loose, long, high-necked dress, and you can come to the party, too. Be sure you get some other women. That's the whole problem." Then he added, "None your age. You're too young."

"For...what?"

"Men."

"I'm eighteen."

"For men my age."

"You keep grinding it in about my being eighteen. That's old enough, even for you."

"Don't push your luck." He indicated she was to climb from the boat to the dock.

She did that and looked back at him. "Pushing luck has to do with gambling, doesn't it?"

"Yeah."

"You think I'm gambling when I'm with you?"

"You have no idea the chances you're taking."

She looked around. "The boat's leaking?"

"It's sound. You're careless in being out at night and away from home."

"I know that. But you'd take care of me."

"I'd fight off other men—"

"See?"

"To keep you for myself." He looked at her so seriously that his eyes were naked.

And she finally understood him. She said, "I'm considering you. But I will not tolerate you being friendly with another woman."

"Okay."

"You can kiss me."

"Not right now."

"You're a nuisance."

And he laughed with great irony. Unfortunately, it was lost on her. He took her hand and led her back to his car.

She lifted her face to the lake breeze and said, "We should have gone out sailing. What a wonderful night."

"It's gonna rain. And if I'd taken you out on the lake tonight, I wouldn't have brought you back. Not for days."

"We'd be wrecked?"

"We'd be distracted from sailing."

"You'd—seduce me?"

"More than likely." He put her into his car and went around to his side.

As he slid under the steering wheel, she said, "We ought to take the kids fishing. I'd like to see if I can cook in a boat."

"You can cook?"

She was honest, "Somewhat."

"You set a great table with cloths and flowers."

She shrugged. "I prefer doing that."

"I can cook."

She grinned at him. "I eat."

"You know I'm retired from the navy?"

"Yes. And you don't have to work. I would like a man around all the time."

"Most women don't. They want the man out of the house, all day, doing whatever will take him away from the house."

"I'd like the company."

"The woman generally has kids."

"Would you ignore children?"

"Do you believe I ignore my three?"

"No. You're very good with them. I especially like the way you teach them. They'll all be good cooks and good mechanics."

"I'd like some land. A farm. A place to give them room enough. They're going to want to drive before it's legal. On a farm, they could."

"A farm." She considered. She was a city woman.

He knew it was so. "We could live as easily on the edge of a big city."

She considered that, too.

"You're very young."

She gave him a look down her nose. "I'm old enough for anything you'd have in mind." He made a sound as if he'd been hit in the stomach. She was alerted, "Are you all right?"

"Not lately."

"Food? Cold? Old war wounds?"

"You."

"I... irritate you?"

"You lure me."

"I do?" She was pleased. "Well, there's a solution for that."

"Do you understand what you're saying?"

"I've invited you to become familiar with me."

He took his foot off the accelerator. "Uh—you *do* know what you're inviting?" He was intense.

"Yes. I like the way you kiss me, and I love having my body against you. And—"

"If you don't want me to wreck this car, you'd better stop right now. I can't handle hearing you say those things and pay attention to driving, too."

She was young. "I... distract you?"

"You're driving me right up my libido and into overdrive."

"You do that with just thinking about sex?"

He told her with great earnestness, "What we'd have wouldn't just be sex, it would be love."

"You love me?"

"Mindlessly."

"Well, I don't think telling me that while we're driving along this way is the right time or place. It's supposed to be romantic."

"You're just lucky I am driving this car along this busy road or you'd be flat on your back and finding out what this is all about."

She wasn't sure. She asked, "You'd be telling me about... what?"

"Are you saying these things just to heat me up?"

"No, I'm curious what you mean."

He was deadly earnest. "I'll have to explain another time. I love you, Felicia. Can you handle that? I'm serious about you."

"Then why did you go out with that woman?"

"Linda. She's really a nice woman. She's older than—"

"If you make one more reference to my age, I'll never speak to you again!"

He glanced over and saw her arms folded beneath her nice breasts, her chin was up. She was looking out the windshield and she was hostile. She was precious. He'd have to quit mentioning how young she was. She was acting her age.

He told her, "I've never slept with Linda Sawyer."

She thought about that, then looked over at him. "Never?"

"Never." And he gave her his honest glance before he looked back to the road.

She considered that for some time. Then she said, "We'll help with the party."

"You'll ask Haw—Emilie to find some women?"

"Yes."

"She's been holding up on her reply until she consulted with you and got your permission?"

"Yes."

"When we're married, are you going to rule me that way?"

"I've only allowed you to tell me you love me. I haven't gone beyond that. Marriage is serious."

"Being in love . . . isn't?"

"I haven't known you long enough to make up my mind as yet. You've mostly avoided me."

"I've avoided *you!*"

"Yes. You've only come over to the house to see me once in all this time."

"Your hawk-eyed aunt wouldn't even let me inside, and you were home and didn't even speak to me!"

"You didn't deserve it. You'd been out with that woman and when I asked how she'd been, you said *great!*"

"I was irritated with you. Because of you, I couldn't enjoy her."

"Ah-*hah!* So you did go out with her to sleep with her."

"No." He was snarling. "I wanted a quiet, adult conversation."

"Baloney!"

Then he smiled like dawn breaking. "You're jealous!"

"Yes!"

And he laughed! How foolish of him.

She tried to get out of the moving car, and he had to steer and keep her arm in his grip as she pushed the door open with her foot and tried to slide out.

Cars honked and swerved, and Salty swerved his car. She was a wildcat. It was then that he said the unpardonable. He said, "Oh, grow up!"

She burst into tears and cried brokenly. He finally turned into Lincoln Park and found a place to park. He was still holding on to her.

He pushed back the seat and pulled her ungently across the console to him. She was stiff and resisting. He curled his body and molded her to him, and he kissed her. It wasn't a killer kiss, but gentle and loving. It was a kiss of timeless love.

She was very emotional—she hiccuped and breathed shiveringly—but she kissed him back. His own eyes were moist, and he groaned with all his emotion.

He growled at her, "Why can't two people come together easier?"

"I don't know. You've been awful."

That made him indignant. "I have!"

"Yes."

"Oh." Now how was he going to tell her he had been trying to be considerate of her because she was so young? Then he remembered stalking her on the stage and, that very night, he had given her the hungriest kiss imaginable out of his frustration, right onstage and in front of all the others. He could hardly mention doing that. He'd had no mercy for her.

He tenderly smoothed her hair back from her face with his big hand, and he felt the wetness of her tears. His heart was mush. He said, "Ah, Felicia. What am I to do about you?"

"Do I have to draw you a map?"

He groaned, holding her furiously to his needy body as he panted, "No." His hands moved and he was greedy. His mouth was devastating to hers, and she exclaimed.

That little sound from her stopped him. He asked, "Did I hurt you?" And he was shocked.

"No. You're just a little rough. I want you sweet and gentle."

"Where can I take you?"

"You need to take me home. Emilie will be worried. She doesn't know where I am."

"She knows you're with me."

"That may alarm her."

"You're not alarmed?"

"I love you."

"Oh, Felicia, you're driving me crazy."

"I'm not doing very well, either."

"I need you."

"Something must be done. I can't stand this. I don't know how to do this."

"I'll figure a way." Then he added in a husky voice, "You're ruining me."

She caressed his scratchy cheek. "I don't want you ruined."

"It'll be all right. I promise."

"What will be all right?"

He replied gently, "Us."

"I've never been part of an 'us' before. I don't know what to do."

In some alarm, he questioned, "You know why men and women marry, don't you?"

With some patience, she half closed her eyes and baited him, "Why?"

He became quite still. "Didn't Haw—Emilie tell you about men and women? About love and babies." He began to sweat. What if she hadn't....

Felicia slid it in, "About the birds and the bees? Which are you?"

He jerked back his head to look at her, and she was grinning wickedly. He replied, "I have to be a bee. I have a stinger."

"I've heard stories about those."

And he asked avidly, "What did you hear?"

"Not enough. I never knew it involved my emotions, or that I could want so badly."

"You...want me?"

"Something's driving me crazy."

He was avid. "That bad?"

And she was honest. "Yes."

He said, "Honey, you've got to get off me and let me out."

"You . . . don't want me?"

He explained, "I have to get out and pick up the car. I won't actually jostle you."

"It will help you? Trying to pick up a car?"

"It's supposed to."

"I'll lift the other side." She slid over the red upholstery to the door and opened it, pushing it again with her feet to keep it open until she could slide out. She met him at the back of the car, and they lifted it. Actually, they only moved the chassis, but she laughed.

He growled, "This is no substitute."

And her glance was compassionate. "It didn't help me any, either."

"Your chatter isn't calming me. Everything you say makes it worse. Are you a tease?"

"How do you mean that?"

"Are you going along with all this to tease me?"

"Going along with all . . . what?"

"Getting out and lifting the car and that stuff?"

"No. I was helping with distracting you."

"You're reminding me of my problem, which is you. You're very alluring."

"I thought you were trying to give me up."

"I was, but you've ruined me. You'll be responsible for me, now, because you prevented my giving you up."

"I'm . . . responsible . . . for you. Honey, as big as you are, no one else can have any control over you, at all."

"You do. You control me."

"I'll drive."

He gave her the keys.

She drove to her house, loving the convertible. "I'll trade you cars."

"I thought the Rambler was H—Emilie's."

"You've got her name down, now, to Hemilie. That's closer."

"I've got to remember not to call her the other name."

"What other name?"

"The one that begins with an *H*."

"I think that would be tactful if you didn't call her that to her face. She's been wonderful to me. She gave up a good man in order to keep me."

"If he'd been a good man, he would have helped to raise you."

"That's what she says, too, but she grieved for him."

"As your dad grieves for your mother?"

"He's never going to get over her. That's why he's trying to help the world. He's just using up his life until he can find her again."

"That's how it would be for me."

Felicia then told him, "I think it's that way for me, too. I really love you."

"How could you keep yourself away from me if you loved me that much?"

She shrugged her shoulders, knowing he was watching, and she said, "I knew everything you were doing, from the boys, and I saw you at rehearsals and could taunt you."

He groused, "So you were deliberately pulling away from my kissing you."

"I was trying to get your attention."

He chided her. "You just about drove me crazy."

"Good."

In a musing manner, he said, "I wonder if you've come under my thumb in time, or if I'll—hush—have to struggle to—be quiet—get you back in control?"

She was flippant as she retorted, "You'll just have to wait and see."

Seven

As Salty drove her home, he told Felicia, "I think I need to talk to Emilie about how rotten you are and what a lousy job she's done raising you."

"You do that, and she'll seal me in a portion of the basement with only a small opening for food."

Salty was doubtful, "She's tough?"

Felicia confirmed it. "You're looking at the ragged child that she sternly raised."

He was glum. "She could have done a better job of you."

"How?"

Salty had no hesitation but instantly replied, "She could have made you docile and obedient." He rolled the car to a stop by her aunt's Nash Rambler and turned to look at his nemesis.

Unfortunately, Felicia laughed such a soft, delightful, teasing laugh. She was outrageous.

So he kissed her. Then he had to force himself to release her, get out of the car and go around to open her door. He extricated her malleable mass from the car and led her to her front door. He patted her bottom as he said, "You're to convince Emilie that she's to bring no less than ten women to my party next Saturday night. Got that?"

And she said, "Yes, master."

"You might be trainable."

She threw her arms around him and gave him a killer kiss that was guaranteed to melt his inner circuits; then she went on into the house and locked the door before he could recover enough to do anything about her.

He stood there in some shock. Where had that child learned to kiss in such a way? They needed to talk about her conduct. He went from the porch and skittered in hit-and-miss stumblings down the steps before going back to his car. He felt he really ought to leave it there and walk home, but it would be too stimulating for her neighbors to have that white convertible parked all night in front of Felicia's house.

He drove home and *then* walked. He found himself almost back to the empty, unlit playhouse before he managed to surface from her killer kiss. He grimly walked back home, thinking of all the lectures he ought to give her, but he knew he would never mention anything about that almost brain-fatal kiss. He might not get another.

The dogs were glad to see him, but they knew enough to simply grin, dance and wag their tails. No one wakened Mrs. T., and the dogs had learned that fast.

Salty went up the stairs and peeked in at the sleeping boys; then he went into his own room, stripped, had an icy shower and went to bed, "to sleep, perchance to dream"? Hell, yes. Terrible, frustrating, hot, wild dreams with Felicia dancing away, just out of reach of his grasping fingers, and she laughed.

The next morning, Salty wakened exhausted. In those last weeks, he had become thinner. More honed. But he looked romantically gaunt.

She came over for lunch. She? What other she was there? He looked at Felicia and smiled. He just smiled.

She moved her head a little, glanced around and looked back at him, and she smiled.

They acted as if they had a silent, secret language. They did. She moved in little wiggles, and he moved in slow nothings, not going anywhere but, with seeming casualness, staying in her way. To get anywhere, she had to go around him. His slow nothings prevented her passing him, until she forfeited a kiss.

She delayed doing that with exquisite timing. She was an actress, after all, and she knew how to handle such a situation.

As she paid the forfeit, the boys appeared and hooted, then jumped around and yelled, "Me, next! Me, next!"

And she laughed because they were still so young they didn't mind being kissed. She looked at Rod, who was almost nine, but she knew it wouldn't be long before he would grin and duck away.

She only petted the dogs.

While Salty finished the preparations for lunch, Felicia set the table very prettily.

She told Salty, "On Saturday, Auntie Em will bring nine women . . . besides herself."

Salty stopped dead in his tracks. "So she'll be here?"

Felicia turned and put one slim hand on her hip and lifted her chin. "And I."

His eyes sparkled with his humor, but his face muscles stayed firm. He said a creditable, "Well, darn. That alters the entertainment altogether."

She moved, straightening things minutely on the table, busy, and her sassy tongue requested, "Just what does that mean? Just what did you have planned to do with my aunt's friends? What scandalous games did you have in mind?"

"Basketball?"

And she laughed.

"You know I put up a hoop for the boys."

She criticized him. "Regulation height."

"They learn. Their eyes learn, and their muscles are pushed. It's good practice. That way as they grow, it's easier."

"I thought only Indiana was basketball crazy."

"We take it to another echelon," he agreed. "It's an established fact that people from Indiana can get to the games in the snow, any kind of snow, but they have to stay there, snowed in afterward. They always go prepared to be snowbound."

"Uh...as I understand it, your people moved to California?"

"Yeah, the burden of being snowbound got to them. It was a matter of pride. They couldn't not go to the games, so they moved to California."

"Why didn't you settle in California?"

"They were gone—from us—by the time I'd reached any thought of actually retiring. The Pacific coast is different. Beautiful to see, but different. The Atlantic coast is tamed. I came here because my best friend, George, lived here. His widow went back home. I miss him very much. He was a good friend and a fine man.

There's a nice bunch of retired navy here. You'll meet some of them Saturday.''

"And Linda."

"Yep." He almost smiled as his kind gaze caressed her. "When you can see past your jealousy, you'll find she's a very nice woman. Your aunt could become her good friend."

"Bosh!"

Salty went to his love and put his hand around the back of her neck to hold her steady and make her face him. "I love you, you little snip. You have no cause to be jealous of any other woman."

She lifted her lashes, and those big eyes were solemn. "I'm not possessive."

His laughter was a rumble in his big chest as he tried to smother it. She immediately tried to release herself from him, but he would not allow that. He pulled her to him and held her. He rubbed his hands on her back and pressed her against his body. He groaned. "You're killing me."

"All I said was that I am not possessive." She was, indeed, snippy.

"Yeah."

Gently, she released herself from him. "Have you contacted the men for Saturday?"

"Yes."

"Are they coming?"

"Yes. Men always show up. Even if it's just for a while. They come in and scan the women, and either stick around or leave. That's why I want you to wear a paper bag over your head. I don't want any of them staying around on the chance you'll notice them." His rasp worsened as he added, "And I don't want you noticing them."

She was fooling with the bouquet on the table and she twitched one flower as she retorted, "I need to look over your friends to see if I approve of them."

He had to tuck his lower lip in quite far and bite on it to stop his laughter. That snip. She was going to censor his contacts? She thought that? Hell, he was going to have to call all those guys and tell them to watch their language—and the jokes.

He looked over at his nemesis. She was worth it.

He looked down her back. "Women's backsides are different from men's."

"It's very rude of you to mention something so personal." Then she asked, "How?"

He was delighted. He cleared his raspy throat and informed her, "Women are different from men."

"You hadn't realized that?"

"I've been—inundated with men for most of my life. I find I made a serious mistake in work choice. I should have chosen more wisely."

Suspiciously, she asked, "Chosen...what?"

He gestured one hand in small, open circles, as if exploring alternatives, and asked, "A female navy?"

"That's just about what I would have expected from you."

"What?" He waited for how she would reply.

"You like women around you."

He could have easily corrected the position, but he let it go. He smiled at his unused words. Instead, he told her, "One woman."

She looked over her shoulder and lifted her eyebrows just a tad. She guessed outrageously, "Mrs. T.?"

"You...you rotten kid."

How could a rasp be so gentle, so loving. Even Salty heard it. It caught him, and he looked at her clearly. God, she was young. She was too young.

Sobered by the thought that continued to intrude, he walked several steps in studied silence, watching the floor.

Felicia immediately felt the change in him. His withdrawal. She watched his subtle distancing of himself, and her eyes narrowed. He was back to rejecting her.

What a nuisance he was. Why couldn't he just accept fate, instead of trying to run his own life his way? Aunt Emilie had told her the difference in their ages would be their biggest problem.

Outside of a gray wig and aging makeup, what was she to do? Tease him into wanting her so madly he would only remember she was female? That seemed a dirty trick. There had to be another way.

She'd known fascination since she'd first heard his rasp in the dark of the theater and was curious to see him. Then he had come up on stage as if he was taking over. He had such an aura of command, of confidence, of control. The male three C's. With women, the three C's were courtesy, consideration and compassion.

A contrast there. Felicia thought she would really like having the command, confidence and control part. She would practice those on Salty Brown. What a basic man he was. And he was much too aware of the difference in their ages. How was she to convince him she was old...enough.

She considered him. It wasn't the lady consideration, it was her own evaluation. She wanted him. He stirred her. He excited her. She wanted him to care for her and about her. How was she going to convince him she was not too young?

She was an actress. She could play a part. She would play that of an older, confident woman. She would fool him into forgetting she was only eighteen. He would know a woman of the world who could handle anything—and him, too.

She had been born under strange circumstances in France, during the last of a terrible war. Her mother had died in a bomb blast that left no real part of her to bury. There was no grave. She and her aunt had had to apply to emigrate to the States. They had to have sponsors to guarantee the country wouldn't have to fund them. They had to get jobs and work. Emilie had done all that. It had taken a while.

And Emilie had loved the man who hadn't wanted to raise someone else's child. That child was Felicia.

Salty said, "What's wrong?"

Felicia turned and looked at him. "I'm plotting how to trap you." She was honest. No sly subterfuge.

His ruined vocal cords said, "Don't scare me that way."

"If you're frightened, I'll take care of you." She turned away dismissively, as if his hesitation was useless.

"How could an almost-woman like you be so sly?"

"I've been through some maturing times. I have reminded myself that I have a strong aunt who was very young when she took the responsibility for me. I've learned to strive for what I need."

"What do you—need." He was serious.

"I shall tell you."

"When?" He was troubled.

"When it's time."

"How will you know that the time is there?"

"I'll know. Then you will."

He was very serious as he considered her. And again, he thought how very young she was.

When their lunch was finished, the boys were resting as they read. At five years of age, John was almost immediately asleep. He was too young to keep up with the older boys. Even barely seven-year-old Mike dozed, but he concealed that quite well. His head would bob and he'd jerk awake and scratch it as if he'd deliberately moved his head that way for that reason.

The porch on the side was closed in long ago. The furniture there was mostly castoff. Nothing matched.

Felicia asked, "Where did you find these things?" and she indicated the furnishings.

"We're looking for a house. I have furniture from several aunts and those from my family that are still stored. We got these to use in this house until we find another that suits us."

"What sort of house and where are you looking?"

He again said, "I'd like the boys to be raised in the country."

She laughed. "So you settle in the middle of a large city to find a country place?"

"Tremont is about in the middle of the world. My parents lived in this area when they started out. I came back here as my starting place. I went to school here. All through school, my friend, George, was a classmate. We joined the navy together. We served together. I thought we'd be friends all the rest of our lives." Salty looked off, remembering.

Then his attention came back to Felicia, and he continued with less nostalgia. "This is a good place. I wouldn't mind staying here, but I'd like to look around and find a place outside the city with some acreage so that we could have chickens, maybe pigs, a cow, that sort of thing. What do you think of that?"

He measured her interest.

"I've never lived in that manner. I've always been in cities. Compared to Paris, Cleveland is a quaint, new city. It is raucous and somewhat raw. Charming."

He guessed, "You don't know how to milk a cow."

She straightened with triumph, lifting out an expressive hand. "A goat! I did milk a goat once." She considered having done such a thing. She shared her experience, "It was—intrusive to do that."

His eyes went to her body, and a shiver went through all his cells. He recognized that what he needed was a distraction from her. Another woman. Naw. It hadn't worked. Linda had been eager and ready. He hadn't wanted her. He only wanted this pre-woman. He was going to have to be firm and forget her. He was going to have to leave her alone.

He began to excuse them from her so that he could get away. "We're going out and—"

"Oh, where are we going?"

She'd very easily included herself. He said, "I've promised the boys we'd do an overnight on the boat." The cabin was very small; she wouldn't be able to go along.

"May I go? Tomorrow is my day off. I've never done an overnight on a boat out on the wide lake. We came on the big boat from Paris. It was wonderful on deck, but our cabin was very small and very crowded. I was young then. It was a great adventure. I would love to go along, if I may?"

How was he to say no? He'd just say it. He said, "The cabin is too small."

"I'll sleep on deck, under the stars! It would be an adventure! Please?"

Damned pushy woman. He couldn't be that close to her overnight. He said, "The boys will—"

"They will love it also. It will be such an adventure. What shall I take? What food?"

"I thought you had a job."

"I do. I work in the mornings from five until noon. That's why I can so easily come by for lunch."

He was shocked. "What do you do?"

"I help at the hospital. I give baths. I'm very good. And I help those who need help with breakfast."

"You work in the women's wards?"

"Not altogether."

He was concerned. "You've been up since five this morning?"

"No. Since four. I must have time to get ready and go. This is summer work. I shall go to acting school this fall. I will be a great actress."

"There isn't much money in acting."

"I shall work for my keep. I'm not greedy. I love pretend. I love to tell stories. Some write them, some tell them, some film them. I act them."

"With rehearsals, when do you sleep?"

"Afternoons. After rehearsals. It's no problem. I don't need much sleep."

"You just catnap here and there?" He frowned at her. "Your body won't take that kind of abuse. You never get into deep sleep."

"I was born during the war in Europe. In my young days, we seldom got to sleep without disturbance. Sleep is taken when it can be had." She shrugged over thinking any other way.

"Come with us." His mouth just went on and said that.

"Wonderful! I will! Thank you. I'll run home and get some things."

"Here." He tossed her the keys. "Take the car. Come back right away."

She grinned at him, looking her eighteen years. She told him, "My aunt will have a fit. She doesn't think I can handle you." She turned and ran from the house, got into his car and drove away with great skill.

Her aunt didn't think Felicia could handle him, but Felicia *did?* Salty was stunned. Which one should he prove was right?

That was a hell of a thing to do to a man. That damned sassy non-woman. Now what was he supposed to do? He was tied up in impossible conscience knots. He was going to have to behave himself? Well, hell.

He could wait and see how serious she would be about good behavior. He could see if she behaved or if she would lead his reluctant steps down the primrose path? Yeah. He'd just wait and see.

But no commitment. He couldn't take on the raising or discipline of a female who was not yet grown and who was in the chancy age bracket, which harbored the luring problem that was Felicia. It was her aunt's problem and it was up to her to stop Felicia from exposing Salty Brown to such temptation.

Within twenty minutes, Felicia was back. She came up the porch steps with vigor and bounce. She wore no bra. She came inside and said, "I left a note."

With that shocking message, Salty knew she did not have her aunt's permission to go on his boat. The harbor police would be out looking for him. He'd have to paint out the name of the boat and rename it. Why would he try to elude the police?

He looked over at Felicia, and he knew why. He'd board the boys in some island hotel and come back for them in a couple of weeks.

They had to be at rehearsals. The play was in two more weeks. They would have to return. Meanwhile, for twenty-four hours, the two fugitives could practice kissing a stage kiss that wouldn't melt all metal within forty feet. How were they going to avoid it?

He sighed. Figuring that out alone would take the entire two weeks. He looked at Felicia in a rebuffing, unfriendly manner, but she was talking to the dogs. Then the boys darted in, dressed for the overnight, and John sweetly leaned against her hip and put his arm around to her other hip.

She was so lithe and clever, she could keep her balance with a little boy doing that, two dogs demanding her attention, and being the subject of the thoughts of a lecherous man. Just the wavelengths of his desire ought to boggle her body.

His eyes took her clothes off her, and his phantom hands explored her roughly. She didn't even notice. She laughed at the boys. She looked up and caught his serious, salacious observation, and her lips parted as she returned his look, very serious and still.

His cells shivered again. He moved and found he actually could. He broke eye contact and looked around, reorienting himself and remembering what he was supposed to be doing.

The dogs had to stay home. He put out food for them because dogs were not any part of Mrs. T.'s agenda, although she would let them outside during the day. Salty saw to it the dogs had water enough in unturnoverable bowls in several places, in case one was stepped in or sloshed over or was impossibly spilled.

And he picked up the packet of clothes he'd gathered for their outing and took them to the car. Then he came back for the sacks of food. They were ready. Was he? He was very unsure.

She and the kids were exuberant. It was the first boat overnight for the kids. He'd never trusted himself— enough—before then. Why did he now? He wasn't sure of that, either.

Well, he'd been trying to get away from the un-woman who haunted him so horrifically. It hadn't been a serious thought to go for an overnight. Any other person would have gracefully withdrawn at his explanation. Felicia had included herself and forced him into doing something he didn't think was entirely safe for the boys to do.

It was still unsafe for the little boys. It was dangerous for him. It was about the most dangerous thing for a grown man that could happen to him. For a grown man, an overnight with an untried woman was treading on disaster.

If he could survive through this, he could handle anything. Maybe even a stage kiss.

He girded his loins and said, "Let's go."

Any man could handle anything for twenty-four hours. As with any crisis, there was a limit. Life did go on. His life would go on beyond this time. It was simply a matter of self-discipline. He had that. In his years as a sailor, he'd proven he was the master of his ship and the captain of his soul...uh...that was, captain of his ship and master of his soul. Whatever...at least up until now.

They went out to the marina and to their boat. There was a small motor to get them out of the harbor and free. The boys wore their vests, and they knew what to do and what not to do. They were efficient. Salty watched them like a hawk.

Felicia sat and was controlled exuberance. She appeared calm in her exchanges with the boys. But Salty was very aware of how excited she was to be there...with him. With him? She didn't pay that much attention to him.

She looked out. She called the boys' attention to various things. She watched exactly what Salty did. In shifting the boom, she said, "I can do that."

But nothing was as easy as when he did it. He allowed her to unwind and rewind the rope as they shifted. And he saw that she watched the boys carefully.

By then, in their inflatable life jackets, the boys had sailed enough to know to be alert and careful. Carelessness was the cause of most disasters. Never walk the edge. Give yourself room. Pay attention.

The boys put their smiling faces to the wind and let their hair blow. They braced their legs and stood steady. They were sailors. He'd trained them well.

They went far out past most of the small boats. They waved at the big ones and looked around.

They dropped a trailing bait into the waters and fished. They laughed at the gulls and birds that came to see what they were doing.

And they ate their supper on deck. They had finger foods and sandwiches, and the kids ate like troopers. As the sun went down and it cooled, there were jackets to put on, and the boys were soon nodding.

So was Felicia. No wonder. With her schedule, sleep had finally caught up with her. They went down to the cabin, put the tabletop between the two sofas and pulled out the sofas into a big bed. They would all sleep together in that crowded space. Sleepily, the boys helped.

Salty went carefully over the rules for abandoning ship. Where and how. Felicia listened. The boys said all the rules along with Salty. They'd had drills. They slept in vests that could be inflated with the flick of a small lever.

Salty turned on a radio to music. It was low and soothing. It was music to sleep by. It was alluring. Who could resist it? Felicia went into the small head, stripped to shorts and a tank top, replaced her own vest and crawled in with the boys.

Salty watched that with very strange feelings. She was on one side of the big, extended bed. On the outside. He was supposed to sleep on the other? Fat chance.

He went up on deck to needlessly see if everything was as it should be. It was. He checked it all seven or eight times. Finally, he could do no more. He yearned to be below with her... and the three boys, of course.

He looked around. There was no need to stay on deck. The running lights were on, they were where they should be. The sail was furled. They were right and tight for the night.

He went below. He sat and watched her sleep. She slept elegantly.

He went back on deck, just to be sure, and sat quietly in the night. Watching. Guarding. Being there. And after some time, she came up on deck.

In the dim reflection of the boat's tiny running lights, she came from the small opening as a Venus from the sea. He thought he was hallucinating. She did all the things his imagination would conjure. She stretched, looked around and saw him. She smiled and came silently to him, her hair being teased by the wind.

She was a sea witch. A danger for a sailor. She would lure him to a watery grave so that she could use his body. Okay. He'd do that. He had to be sure the boys were safe; then she could have him.

She said, "An iron man."

He couldn't figure that out. He sat, waiting for her to indicate what he should do.

She sat beside him just like any mortal woman. "I brought you some coffee. Must you keep watch?"

She was mortal?

She looked around. "It seems so peaceful, so wonderful. Is there any danger?"

None to the boat, just to him. Felicia. She was the danger.

Eight

Salty looked past the tiny lights that outlined his boat, and his gaze went on to the magical twinkling stars. He remembered being shocked that those weren't pasted on the sky's ceiling. The lights were other suns that were distances so far that it boggled the mind.

And he looked on his love. How could he bring himself to shun her? Couldn't he do that for her sake? She was so young. Perhaps he could become an uncle to her children after she married a more suitable man.

But the thought of seeing her with another man who loved her and had access to her, squirmed in Salty's soul. Worse, he groaned in muffled anguish.

She turned instantly to him. "Are you ill?"

His rasp was rusty. "I'm sick with love."

She was very serious. "There is a cure to that."

"You're too young." He gave her up. He declined her tentative offer. He felt noble and devastated. Torn. Anguished. Unsure. He looked at her, squinting his eyes at her halo of purity.

She said quietly, "I'm not a virgin."

He was jolted so that he thought a storm had just announced itself. He looked quickly at the stars and frowned, then understood what she had said. "Who."

How like a man to have to know who was the other man. Not the circumstances. Only who he was?

"In Paris, it was long ago. I was almost Rod's age. He was kind. It was interesting. While he was grown, he wasn't large. He was concerned for me. I felt no shame. It was quickly over, and he was gone."

"Where was Emilie?"

"Working. So was I. I was selling tiny baskets of little silk flowers on the street. He had me go into the alley with him so that he could take the money from his shoe. He gave me five francs. He forgot the basket."

"What did Emilie say?"

"I never told her."

"You were ashamed?" Salty's concern was poignant. "It wasn't your fault!"

"No. I remember being sorry for him. No. Really. He was distressed. In that time, there were few condoms available even on the illegal black market. The Church was severe. He did not harm me. He did a forbidden act. And he suffered for it."

Earnestly trying for his understanding, the eighteen-year-old Felicia spoke carefully in order to instruct a retired sailor who was thirty-eight. "Everyone has a limit for their endurance—" she gestured in searching for clarity "—of pain, truth, shame or stress. Some people's limits come sooner than others. Some endure. Some cannot. You never hear of the survivors. Their lives go on."

She shrugged minutely over human frailty. "While I was very serious over the encounter in the alley, I knew it would only distress Emilie, who was already pushed with the responsibility of me. I did not tell her.

"I was young, but I knew much from watching people. Children had nothing to compare to what they had. To them, life was normal. Children grow up more quickly in such times.

"Even in the survivors, there are different levels of reactions to endurance, to ambition... to stress. Some survive, some recover over time and some do not."

Felicia looked out over the seemingly endless, clean lake. "In all times, there are people who deal with stunning things." Thoughtfully, she moved one hand in small gestures as she defined them, "Helping in a struggling country. Helping with a failing business. Helping a struggling friend.

"Then there are those who survive the loss of a loved one, a lost business or a job that was all they had." She hesitated as she considered. "While there are the defeated ones, there are those who can put defeat aside without being crippled. They are the survivors.

"People react differently. Stress is everywhere, in varying degrees all of the time, for one reason or another. Some are motivated by it. They find it a challenge and search for a solution. There are those who cannot. Some people's strength can be in another area of their personality.

"I was not harmed by the alley experience in Paris. I was not shamed by it. I don't know why it is so, but so much was going on at that time. The residue of the war was terrible. People were hungry and homeless. There was severe rationing.

"In the villages, the returning men took the women who'd lain with German soldiers. The women were stripped of their clothes and their money taken. Their heads were shaved. Wearing only their shoes and carrying a purse, the naked women were forced to leave the town and find another place.

"The men allowed the camera. It was documented. I have seen it on TV these years later. But the naked women walked away with their backs straight and their heads high.

"Other women, in sympathy, began a 'fad' for short short hair. Emilie was one. So was I. We were of the survivors."

"Yeah." Salty took her small hand into his large, roughened one. He saw beyond his boat and into another time. "What you say is like it was for us, except that we were on board ship and mostly clean and food was no problem. There was discipline.

"We had guys on board that were like you said. They saw only the wide deepness of the uncontrollable ocean. To them, it was filled with danger and the dark unknown. We teased them, but they clung to the ship like holding on to a floating log. There were guys who transferred out, but there were the other guys who stayed on board. People are different.

"There were guys who got dizzy just looking over the ship's side down to the water. They laughed at themselves. Most of the men that came back from the wars could pick up their lives and go on, but there were men that couldn't.

"Some saw horror in the night fighting attacks." Salty was silent as he saw it in his mind. Then slowly, he said, "If you could ignore the fact that there were people in the place that was being bombarded, the shell flights and their burstings were beautiful. Like a Fourth of July display."

After a slight pause, Salty said, "Some watched the kamikaze, the Jap suicide planes, in trapped terror but others were challenged to defend the ship."

Felicia commented gently, "You were one who took it as a challenge."

"Naw. I was half as—some of each. But the ship was our base. It needed all us little ants to protect her."

"Then perhaps you do understand?"

"Yeah." He was so serious.

"I was not harmed."

Salty looked at the nubile witch whom he loved. His raspy voice was blurred. "Why did you tell me?"

She was practical. "Because you want me, but you aren't sure you should make love with me. Making love with me won't change me. I want you. Salty, please."

He groaned and brought her hand to his mouth to press it there. His body burned with his heat. He wanted her so badly. But some small caution made him gasp and try for some discipline. "Felicia. You don't know what you're doing to me."

"Why do you think I came along? I could hardly seduce you with Mrs. T. there at your house. You do remember how Emilie was when you fixed my car? She didn't let up for even one minute. When you said you were coming on the overnight, this was the only way I could figure out. I needed to corner you. On land, you get away. Here, you're limited on how far you can run, and you'd never be so crass as to waken the boys and yell for their help."

She was teasing him! She was making this heavy temptation into light fun. She was inviting a romp on a sailboat deck. There were cushions. What was he thinking?

Yes.

She was going on. "I love the way you kiss me. I love your body. You are just beautiful. I want to love you. I want release. I've been so aching with need of you. I know what I ask. I have done it. It would not surprise me or shock me."

"You were so young!"

"Love me. I will not be changed."

"He was a rat. Shame to him."

"He was already shamed."

"How could you know something so well at such a young age?"

"I was there. Children are observers. You give them good guidelines and they become good people. You do wonderfully with your sons. What would you do with daughters?"

"They'll probably learn basketball."

"You'll have daughters?"

"I need a wife first."

"I'd like little girls as sisters for your sons."

"Are you proposing to me?"

"You don't appear to know how to propose to me. You pull back twice for each time you advance. You frustrate me."

"I can't begin to tell you how much you frustrate me."

"I can soothe that. I have condoms with me in my pocket. Let me. Kiss me. Hold me. Love me."

She reached across his chest to put her hand on the other side of his head to gently turn his face to hers. Then she kissed him. There in the night's blanket of stars twinkling back at the outline of lights on their small shell in the middle of the black water, she kissed him.

It was as if they were alone in the universe. They were Adam and Eve. In all of space, only they existed.

His hunger was so tightly controlled that she was stimulated unbearably. She wasn't sure he would make love to her. He had too much control. She squirmed to get her body closer to his, making him shudder and shiver in his restraint. He gasped and his mouth was opened to aide in his try for oxygen. He was pitched almost to desperation.

But he did have a couple of brain cells still working. His rasp grated, "I have to close the doors."

She looked around the small, pin-lighted boat and thought he'd slipped a cog. She pulled back to look at him and saw that he was struggling for determination to leave her!

What doors?

He was rejecting her? She couldn't believe it. He wasn't made of steel. Maybe iron. That rasp. But how could he kiss her as he did and decline to make love with her? Maybe he . . . couldn't? How could he kiss that way and not feel some attraction? He acted as if—

He'd struggled to his feet, and she watched in dismay as he walked carefully away from her. He went to the opening of the cabin, closed those doors, took some bells from the side of the cabin and looped them over the doors.

He turned and looked right at her. He would come to her. He would come to her and make love to her. He had only needed to know if the boys wakened and came on deck. He was responsible. He was perfect. He would love her. He would admit that he loved her and he would tell her so.

Her eyes were so big that she looked like a magical night's dream. A wanton woman who lured men to their

destruction. Could he survive her? If he loved her this
night, there on the boat, could he go on with his life as
a normal man? What magic was this? What lure?

By then he was back on the small seat at the back of
his small boat, and he was seated beside her in that
space. The rudder was tied at rest. The water moved
softly, in a lulling way, easing him, making him feel
soothed.

How could he be soothed when he was afire? He had
turned to iron and his body was encased in steel from his
heat. He could harm her if he didn't move carefully and
touch her gently.

He gathered her against his hard surface and his
breaths were scalding steam. He said, "Felicia."

She made a feline, purring throat sound and said,
"Yes."

A corner of his mind wondered if she was agreeing
that was her name? Or was she agreeing to his making
love with her? She was not resisting him. Her arms were
around his shoulders; her hands were in his hair; her
mouth was soft on his chin.

He kissed her.

It was like always. Chaos. He shivered and shuddered and gasped. He fed on her mouth as if he'd die
without it. He needed her. He wanted her. He groaned
and swallowed and held her close, and he said her name
quite a number of times.

Her husky laugh was deep in her throat and it lifted
his hair. She was ready for him. He moved his hands on
her body, and she was soft and marvelously made. Her
body moved in small writhings against his. She ran one
hand down his chest and smoothed it over the expanse
of it, then it went to his belt—and—she—unbuckled—
it. Then she began to run down his zipper!

His rasp fogged, he said, "Slow down. I'm trying for control."

And *she* said, "Not this time."

He whooshed out air and, without that oxygen, he became a little lightheaded. He trembled and his hands shook. "Felicia." He said her name yet again.

She loved it. She moved her shoulders and rubbed her body against his, and she moved her face over his like a female cat in heat.

He said her name some more. His hands were rigid and careful, his breaths were ragged.

She wiggled free of him, moved the seat padding off onto the deck and lay down with her body on that. She opened her arms to welcome him. He was stunned. He was on overload. He was unsure. He was mad with desire. He carefully ripped off his turtleneck shirt and shed his shoes before he pushed down his pants and got rid of them. He crouched down beside her.

In her softened voice, she suggested, "Undress me."

That made him react like a bucket of hot water thrown on a freezing man. He was awkward but persevered, and he unsheaved her wondrous body from the covering garments...whatever they'd been. And he looked at her.

She watched him, looking at him, but mostly watching his reaction to her and his body's need.

With some hesitation, she said, "You're not little."

He instantly curled down beside her as he urgently reassured her softly, "Neither are you. It'll fit just right."

"I probably should have seen you before I made this offer. I had no idea you would be ... so ... big."

He put his big, hard hand on her soft stomach and moved his hand in a wonderfully soothing way. He looked at her and watched his hand. But he was stalled.

"I'm just like any other woman."

"No. You're you. You're Felicia. My Felicia."

"Have I entrapped you because you want me so much and I'm willing? Is that all it took to make you claim me?"

"I claimed you all along. I've been possessive of you ever since I saw you sitting on the stage, reading and using that voice of yours to lure me like a siren."

"A fire siren?"

"One who lures sailors."

"As a sailor all those years, have you met very many sirens?"

"You're my first."

Her laughter was soft and disbelieving.

He clarified it. "I have had a woman or two, but they weren't sirens. They were women. Normal, ordinary women. You are not."

"What's the difference?"

"They were mortal."

"So am I."

"No, you're the one Homer wrote about. You're the one they've all written about. You're immortal and dangerous for mortal men."

"I'll be careful of you."

"I love you, Felicia. You're too young for me."

"Not ... too ... young."

"This is a gift, to let me have you, but I can't marry you. You're mine for now, but I must not keep you. It would be like caging a wild bird. We'd both die. I must let you go."

"You have a wonderful imagination. I'm a human woman. I shall grow old and become feeble and disinterested."

"No."

She shrugged. Beautifully. She had distracted him. He forgot their conversation.

She told him, "If you will make love with me, you can be cured of your curiosity and free of me."

"I don't believe that's so."

"We could try?"

He kissed her marvelously, breathing harshly and trembling, his hot hands seeking her gently. "If I make love to you, how can I remember the kids are sleeping below deck? How can I know we haven't all drowned and I have been allowed this incident because God knows I can't ever make heaven, but I've done one or two things that gives me this reward before I go to hell?"

"We can see." Then she had to ask, "What wicked things have you done?"

"This is one." He kissed her exquisitely.

As soon as he lifted his mouth, she asked, "Who were the others?" Not 'what' but who.

"I don't recall any other woman."

"Then you're probably okay. We're alive, the boat is still buoyant, the boys sleep peacefully and all is well."

"Not . . . yet."

And she laughed a low throat sound that curled his toes but made everything else hard and tense.

He kissed down her body, slowly and quite moistly.

She inquired, "I didn't know that wickedness was a part of this."

"Yes."

"What else?" She was a little sassy.

"You're supposed to caress me."

"Your hair?"

"Lower."

"Your mouth?"

He moved his head down to salute her nipples. He said a guttural, "Lower."

She moved her hands down to his chest. "Yours is different."

He lifted his mouth to tell her, "Lower."

She stroked the silken hair on his stomach and chuckled. "I love this. It feels so wonderful."

He rubbed her stomach and agreed.

She murmured with her eyes slitted, her lips parted and her teeth closed as if experiencing exquisite pain.

He said, "Lower."

"Is that the only word you know?"

"Right now. The suspense is killing me."

"You...want me to touch you...there?" And she touched him.

"Oh, yes..." He writhed.

"You're very strangely built."

"The word is not 'strange' but 'perfect'."

"I'm unsure."

"I'll show you." He shifted and hung above her. "Open your knees."

"That seems a rash thing to do."

He smiled. "You'll love it." He urged, "Open your knees."

"How much?"

"Wide enough for my hips."

"Ah. So that's the way it is. Uh, can you... Oh. Ah. Uh...uh...oh. Yes." Then she relaxed and sighed, "Ah. Um. Yes."

But where she thought they'd managed quite well, he was in worse shape than ever. He sweat. He groaned. He moved minutely, controlled harshly and he shuddered.

She asked, "What's the matter?"

"I don't think I can wait."

That was strange. "For what?"

"To come."

"Where?"

"You haven't been loose and running around for very long. I need to move. Are you all right?"

"Move...where?"

"Like...this." And he did very carefully move. Then he pulled from her and said, "I don't have a condom!"

"Oh," she replied efficiently, "In my shorts pocket. I brought some along because I was determined you wouldn't shut me out."

"*I* would...shut *you* out... You are a strange woman."

She was busily reaching for her shorts and feeling in the pockets. She said, "These were all they had."

"Five? *Six?* You have a wonderful opinion of me."

"I wasn't sure I could get one on you, right, the first time. I tried some on a carrot. You're a different size. I'm not sure these will work. They could be too tight. Would that hurt?"

"I don't think so."

"Let me."

"No. Let me. If you start fooling around with me, now, I'd probably ruin everything."

"How?"

"I'm very pitched. I could go off like a skyrocket."

"If you do that—inside me—would it hurt me?"

"No. It'll feel good."

"This is much more complicated than that first time—"

"I'd rather not be compared to a child molester."

"I was big for my age. I was almost as tall as—"

"I really can't handle thinking about that now. Talk to me about how you are feeling about me and about doing this with me."

"Well, you are bigger."

"I want to hear how much you like doing this with me."

"I don't know, yet."

He stopped rolling on the condom and looked at her. "Are you a cold woman?"

"I don't know."

"Well, I've seen you react *very* well to my kissing you. You're a hot woman. So quit chattering and help me a little by moving and wiggling and pretending you're excited. I'm about to go out of my mind. I've never seen a woman so chatty at a time like this, and to compare me to another man is rude."

"Oh."

"Tell me you like me." He lay on her again and sought entrance.

She put her hand down to find him and guide him. She was saying, "You're a very strange person and you really are unpredictable. You walk like a very dangerous ma—" She gasped at his entrance.

He growled in his rasp. "That isn't romantic! Tell me something nice!"

"Oh . . ." She shivered and rubbed her hands up his sides as she slid her feet along his legs. She said, "You scare my insides like riding on a roller coaster."

"I do?"

"Yes. And— Oh, I like that. Do that some more. Ah, yes... I...umm. Oh... Ssssalteeee. Um... Wiggle that way again. Um, yes, push. Ah. Oh. Umm. Salty, how I love you."

"You love me, really?" He had paused before moving slowly, braced on his elbows, watching her face.

Her eyes were closed and her chin was up. Her mouth was open and her shoulders moved as she tried to move her hips under his weight.

He moved a little, watching her face.

"I like that. Do it again."

He became so involved with watching her and pleasing her that he wasn't as hurried as he'd been, and he took her very slowly to ecstasy and rode the wild winds with her. The winds took them to paradise.

When they were a collapsed heap of wrung-out flesh lying on the deck again, they murmured. Their hands petted each other minutely.

He managed to swivel his head and look at the closed doors to the cabin. They were still closed, and he'd heard no bells.

He looked down at the sated woman under him. He was braced on his elbows, and her smile of fulfillment was fulfilling to his soul. He had pleased her. How often did a couple reach that summit together? Not that often. Generally one or the other was left behind. They'd hit the heights together their first time!

First time? That sounded as if he planned to continue to make love with her. Hadn't he decided to give her up? Well, they could be friendly until he found her another man.

Another man? And he recognized that he could never turn her over to anyone else. That meant that he'd have to leave Cleveland and go somewhere else. He couldn't witness her becoming interested in any other man ... to see her smile at another man ... or touch one.

What a terrible thing to be thinking of having to separate from her entirely, when he was still embedded in her hot sheath, having shared the heights with the semi-woman. How could he leave her?

By being firm. Knowing that he must. He was too old for this beginning-woman. She was too many years and experiences younger than he. He was wicked and selfish to have allowed himself to be lured by her into this wondrous coupling. He had no excuse for his conduct except his—want.

And he understood, then, that he would have her again. And again. As long as she would allow him to make love with her.

What had he done?

She moved and stretched out her arms and legs while still lying under his body, and she made contented sounds. He listened to every one, allowing her contentment to soak into his memory. His memory? He would be able to remember this night all the rest of his life.

"How soon can we do it again?"

He couldn't laugh. He bent his head down and kissed her shoulder. The rumble of his humor was gentle and soft. "You're a sex fiend?"

"You don't appear to mind. Aren't you—supposed—to deflate." Her intimate muscles squeezed him.

He gasped in shocked surprise. Well, perhaps not shocked surprise as much as stimulated delight? She did it again and he said, "Careful."

"Why should I be careful...now?"

"Have I finally found an insatiable woman?"

"I'm not sure. We could find out. Do you need another condom?"

"Yeah."

"Well, darn. I thought we could just move around a little and see if we could get you interested enough to love me again."

"I—" But he couldn't give her words like those. He didn't dare. He was too old for her. Maybe not right then, but in ten years he would be almost fifty, and she wouldn't yet be thirty. That was sobering.

He needed to protect her from himself.

Tomorrow. He'd begin to do that tomorrow. It would be soon enough, and he would have had a night of love with this scandalously sensual woman.

"What are you doing?" he asked his one-night stand.

"You did that to me."

"Well, yes, but I don't believe you should...ah... You witch! Not there, you...ah... Yes. Lower."

She pushed with her body and one foot to roll him onto the plank deck. Then she leaned over him to explore him at her leisure. "One nice thing about you being disinterested, is that I can have the freedom of you this way. I can see how you're made like... Well, this is interesting. The sperm are in these?"

"Yeah. They were."

"And they go into here?"

"Careful."

"Let's take this one off. It's full. We'll put another one on."

"We?"

"It's a new skill." She was busy. "I need to know how to do things."

"Not that. Here, I'll do it."

"You're so selfish! It's rude to be that selfish."

"I'll let you do it as soon as I can. But you need some training...first."

"What sort of training."

"I need to rinse off."

"If you go inside, you might wake the boys."

"I'll go over the side."

"No!"

"It's okay. I've swum in the middle of the ocean. This is tame in comparison."

"I said, no, you may not go over the side into the water at night. I've said this."

"Why... not?" He was vulnerable.

"I don't know how to get the boys back to shore."

He said a flat, disappointed, "Oh." What had he expected? He knew they weren't suited. Why had he expected and anticipated a commitment from her when he was withdrawing from her?

She said, "Throw the bucket over, and I'll rinse you myself."

It was worth the effort. That would be worth any effort. He managed to get his sated body organized and heaved up to stand and reorient himself. No one was anywhere around them. He went to the stern of the boat. The bucket was on a rope and he eased it over to fill it and brought it back up dripping.

He set it on the deck. She brought his shirt over and dipped it into the water. "Sit down on the deck. No. Over there. I don't want to walk in the water and then get into bed with wet feet."

They would sleep? Before that comment, she had sounded as if she planned a night of love. Then he thought of all the time she'd given him in the last weeks, when she should have been sleeping. She was probably exhausted. She'd already endured him once.

She hadn't really—endured. She'd appeared to love making love with him. Of course, she was an actress. Maybe she was actually a cold woman. She'd given a good performance. She'd fooled him into thinking she liked having sex with him.

No. They'd made love.

She couldn't have learned to fake all those movements and sounds. She was only a budding woman. And old Hawk Eyes, who went by the gentle name of Emilie, wouldn't have allowed her to be so experienced that she could fool a sailor.

They'd really made love. She'd liked making love with him. And he was glad he'd known her so intimately before he had to give her up.

She washed his body with his T-shirt. She stroked him. She felt with her hands to be sure he wasn't sticky. And she lifted parts and cleaned him.

In all his knowledge, she was the first woman to do so. The time he was wounded, and when his jeep was wrecked and he was helpless, there'd been male orderlies who weren't especially gentle, but they had been considerate.

This was different. This was heaven. This was killing! This was...enticement. This was won-der-ful. This was a man's dream.

"You know what you're doing to me. You can see for yourself."

"It's nicely washed. Let's put it back."

He was dreaming?

She took his hand and led him back to the pads lying on the deck. He trailed along like a tamed man. He smiled. He wasn't the least bit reluctant. He wasn't adult enough to put a stop to something he knew she shouldn't do again. He just went right along and participated.

He laughed in his throat very softly. The pleased sound shivered in Felicia. She loved it. She hugged him to her nakedness and she laughed with him.

How marvelous was love. How foolish he'd been reluctant. How wonderful to have her curl around him and give him such pleasure. How amazing.

And with their repletion, he again pried himself from her to go again and draw up a pail of lake water.

But it was he who washed her, and he who dried her, and he who pampered her. He was gentle and sweet. And he kissed her sipping kisses that wouldn't arouse him, but they did.

And she saw that he wanted her yet again, but that he paid no attention to his leaping sex. He was simply gentle and sweet to her, caring for her.

He led her down the steps to the cabin. The boys lay soundly sleeping. And he moved them gently to give her room. Then he kissed her yet again, and she crawled onto the bed, to curl down and sigh as she smiled up at him in the darkness of the starlit cabin.

She relaxed and soon her breathing was steady.

He figured she must be very tired that she could sleep so quickly. He should never have encouraged her sassy flirting that second time. He should have let her go to sleep then.

When the boys wakened in the morning, Salty hushed them. He took their breakfast up on deck and fed them there. He wouldn't allow them to go back into the cabin to the head. He taught them to relieve themselves over the side. "It's a big lake."

And she slept.

They finally docked about four that afternoon, and they wakened her gently then. The boys were as gentle with her as their dad. They didn't shout or rough her or laugh, they were as gentle as one is with a little child.

She stretched, and the males all watched with gentle smiles. Salty saw that. They loved her, too.

Nine

It was during that time when Salty's sons began to learn their care and gentleness for women. Felicia smiled at them, and they turned their faces to her as to the warming sun.

At the marina, they cleaned and straightened the boat. They carried the sheets and towels and garbage back to their car.

Before Salty took Felicia home, they stopped for supper at a McDonald's, the new, proliferating fast-food chain which sold hamburgers for fifteen cents apiece.

As he escorted Felicia to her door, Salty was conscious of the fact that the boys were deliberately in the car. He didn't want any of Felicia's neighbors to think the outing had been a pairing. The boys had been along.

Filled with the quick supper, nicely tired by their adventure, the boys lounged in the car lazily. Had they been fresh, they'd have been sitting on the seat's edge and watching around. Salty knew that and had used it to protect Felicia.

Emilie was at the door. She opened her mouth—Salty said, "Come meet my boys."

"I met them when you fixed my car."

"Ah, yes. Felicia is a good sailor."

Emilie's eyes narrowed. "Obviously, so are you."

Now how was Salty to take that? His boat handling? A marauding invasion? An intrusive presence?

Salty smiled as if complimented. "We'll expect you and your friends on Saturday. Come early and get acquainted with our house."

She viewed him as if he was a really awful snake. She only narrowed her eyes. She did hesitate. She was considering taking the broom and clearing him off her porch. But she wanted to go to the party because she'd already invited all those other women. How could she back out then? She gave him one silent nod and turned away.

Felicia's eyes sparkled with hilarity. She'd watched her aunt and knew every nuance. She said to Salty, "Thank you for a marvelous cruise."

"Thank you for being such a good...sport."

She narrowed her own eyes, just like her aunt had done, but her narrowing was wicked. "You're welcome."

Those were the words she used.

Salty's lips parted with his barely controlled gasp. She was too young to be that bold. She was being polite.

She added, "Any time."

She moved that pliant, naughty body around the barely opened screen door and into the house. She glanced back over her shoulder and said, "I'll probably...see...you soon?"

His own body went into some kind of sexual shock. He nodded, absently distracted by such waves of sensualism that he turned away to wave his arms and fight for balance, as he manipulated trying to control those treacherous porch steps, yet again.

At the bottom, he turned and looked at the steps. They were only steps. No, they were the steps to and from Felicia.

He called Felicia that evening, but Emilie answered their phone and said Felicia was sleeping.

He paced a long time, thinking of her lying in bed, alone and asleep. He'd wakened how many times in the night and seen that she was actually there, on the other side of three sleeping boys. She had been there. It hadn't been some magic dream.

She'd been with him. She'd bathed him—

Salty stopped like an abandoned marionette hung from a string at the back of his neck, his head down, his arms loose, his knees unreliable.

His eyes closed and his hands slowly curled and came to his chest to spread there as he moved them down his body to his thighs. He silently groaned. How was he to give her up?

She came dancing in the next noon. And Salty could only stare as if the world had been dark and dreary, and now there was light. She greeted them all and laughed. She cast flirting glances his way as she replied to the exuberant boys.

They were teasing her about sleeping through all of yesterday and missing all the fun.

She laughed and was so amused, she couldn't not smile, but she blushed in a wonderful pinkening that charmed her male audience.

In surprise, Rod told his father, "She's blushing. Why is she blushing?"

"She's glad to see us."

"She's never been that pink before." Rod looked at her, puzzled, smiling very similarly to his father.

She put her hands to her face and chided, "You're not supposed to call attention to the fact that I'm embarrassed."

John had to know what the word meant. They explained she was shy.

Mike only smiled amid the chatter. He volunteered, "She was up on deck with Salty."

That stilled the adults.

"They talked." He turned and shared a look with Salty.

He asked Mike, "How do you know?"

"I heard you guys talking. And I heard her laugh."

Carefully Salty said, "I didn't see you come up on deck."

"I was in bed."

The two guilty ones exchanged a sober look.

Mike added, "She's got a nice laugh." And he looked at the sober, pink-cheeked woman who had rather bigger eyes.

That night was their first full rehearsal. It was for timing. And it was a little sloppy. Joe watched the lovers in advancing their heightened awareness and frowned. He was thoughtful, or was it that he was puzzled?

The next night was chaos. Everybody seemed to forget their lines, or where they were supposed to be, or they got mad and lost their tempers.

Joe was tolerant. "You're being a bunch of prima donnas—sorry, ladies, there's no male counterpart for that. You're getting the jitters. No need. You'll be brilliant. This is part of the process. You'll do better tomorrow. Felicia, you're so perfect, you scare me."

And those words settled into Salty without any trouble at all. The words just made themselves comfortable and began to eat at his conscience. She could be a great actress.

Why should that bother him? He was giving her up. He wouldn't be in her way or trying to lure her from a great career.

If he was serious about her, on that improbable scenario, he was unhampered. He could go wherever she was needed. It would be no big deal.

What about the boys?

They would need security. They would be in school. He could not board them out.

Well. Business people traveled. There were families in the navy who were separated while the husbands had been to sea. Separations could be adjustable.

Why was he considering her career as a problem for him?

It wasn't one. She was free.

He didn't take her home after rehearsal, not right away. He drove her to the closest park and parked. He told her, "You have to consider becoming a star."

"I'm going to begin my degree this fall. That's why I'm working. And I have a scholarship."

"I didn't know that."

"Yes. I was fortunate. The other contenders were impressive."

"No one can touch you. You're remarkable."

"I'm—a little uneasy with the opening. I have never before been on the stage alone. I have a little trouble not being overly aware there'll be an audience."

"I was in your audience."

"Yes. But I knew you were there. I 'played' to an invisible man."

"How'd you know I was there? You couldn't see me."

"I knew. I always know. I always will."

"Now, Felicia, you also have to know that I'm too old for you."

"You kept up fairly well."

"There's nothing to compare to a smart-mouthed woman."

"You like my mouth."

"Damn you," he groaned and put his head in his hands.

"We'll be through with Saturday's rehearsal in time for the party. Emilie will come early, if you'd like her to. To be sure someone is there if anyone comes early."

"That's kind of her." And he wondered if she and Mrs. T. would go through all his drawers. They would never find his new cache of condoms. So. He had gotten them. He planned for more loving encounters with this budding woman? Yeah.

He said, "You ought to kiss me."

She flirted. "Why?"

"Because you haven't in much too long a time. Get yourself over here."

"Why did you buy a car with bucket seats?"

"I didn't know I was going to meet you and get to fool around with you."

"Oh? Are we going to 'fool around' tonight?"

"I sure hope so."

She slid over the console, and he tucked her close, as she asked, "Where does it hurt?"

"Now, how did you know that?"

"Anybody who needs attention generally hurts. Like John with his knee."

"My *knees* are all right. I have no problems with knees or elbows."

"You have another problem?"

He said, rather ponderously, "I need to be kissed."

"Oh, is that all? I can handle kissing you."

But she couldn't. She pushed against his eager body and groaned and gasped and wiggled and drove him crazy. He had to be crazed. *Something* was making his hands desperate and his body curl that way.

The park was patrolled. There was no place to go. They were about as frustrated as two people could get. He said, "We'll find a place."

"Let's go to your boat."

He was shocked.

"You took me there once. Why not again?"

"It's the same guard. He'll know."

"I don't mind his knowing."

"He might try for you."

"He's too old."

Salty became silent. He said sadly, "So am I."

She laughed. She laughed and put her hands on his ears and kissed him; then she moved impossibly in that limited space and put her hand on him.

He about went through the roof of the convertible. He said, "You're wicked. You just about shot me through the roof, doing that."

"This?"

He gasped and shuddered. "Now look what you've done."

"Why do you have the top up on this car on a wonderful night like tonight?"

"I didn't want anyone being able to see inside too easy."

"Oh? What had you planned on doing to me?"

"Like now." His hands moved on her.

"I love you, Salty."

"Naw. I've just caught your attention, you hot woman. You'll drain me and then start looking around for a new stud."

"No."

"You wanta move into my house?"

"Emilie would send me to a convent."

"That would be nasty."

"Yes. So therefore, I'm circumspect."

"You know a word like that?"

"I had it drilled into my head from birth."

"By Emilie?" he guessed.

She agreed, "By Aunt Emilie."

"She's a good woman."

"I told her so, and she cried."

"You must have been a handful all her life."

"Practically all, but I've been darling and very ladylike, until just recently."

"What happened just recently?"

"You."

"Aw, honey, you know this'll never work. You need to fly to the moon, you're so talented."

"Are you trying to discourage me?"

It took him a while, but he finally said, "Yeah."

"You don't want me?" She waited.

"You're wonderful, Felicia, but I'm too old. You're on the very brink of your life, and, honey, it could be fantastic."

She replied quite emphatically, with marvelous, young confidence, "I expect it to be fantastic. But it'll be my way."

"You'll be going to school. You'll be very busy."

"Yes."

"You need to concentrate on your schooling. You don't need any distractions."

"You're not a distraction. You've become a necessity."

"You're a hungry woman?"

"I'm a loving one. I love you."

"Aw, Felicia. If you act that way, how can I be noble and give you up?"

"No way."

At his age, he could find no way to make love to her. It was maddening. It was late. She needed to get home and get to sleep.

He took her home . . . to her own house. And he released her to go inside. Going back down those slippery stairs was as tricky as ever, and he went to his own house.

There he paced and sorted out problems, and he faced the fact that he would have her for a while but that, eventually, he must give her up. He must never mention marriage or permanence.

Being a man was tough. It required being honorable and honest. That was discipline. But those traits would require that he release Felicia. And doing that was going to be worse than anything he'd ever had to do in all his life. It could sunder him.

How could he survive?

* * *

The next rehearsal was ragged for the third time. Joe got mad and read them all the riot act. He told them the problem was that they were all capable of doing better. They *had* done better! What in hell was the matter with them? They acted like a bunch of amateurs. He was disgusted!

He shouted at them. He never shouted. He was a mild gentleman. He shouted that while they were all anonymous, he was a known director. They were ruining his reputation. That's what he got for fooling around with charities.

And he said if they didn't shape up by Saturday, he was going to lock the door and keep them all there until they did it right!

Felicia said, "I have a job."

Joe looked at her and retorted, "If I have to stay here with these blundering buzzards, then you have to also. Be quiet."

Salty rasped, "Joe—"

And Joe said, "You're the worst of all! What the hell's the matter with you? You've turned into a zombie!"

Salty just looked at Joe. Everyone was silent.

Joe said, "Aw, go home and go over your stuff. Then come back tomorrow like you know what you're doing here. Git!"

Then he said, "Salty, I'd like a word with you."

So Salty stayed like a recalcitrant kid who's been told to stay after school.

Joe lit a cigarette.

Salty commented, "I thought you quit."

"Be quiet."

"Now, Joe—"

"You've lost the tension. It just occurred to me, not five minutes ago, that you're sleeping with her. You don't have that edge. You're relaxed and you already know you have her. You're ruining my play."

"No." He denied that flatly. He explained, "I recognized that I can't keep her."

"Well! Use *that!* Give the tension back to us, damn it. Give me back the prowling tension that makes this whole damned play."

"Yeah." And with some bitter irony, Salty quoted, *"The play's the thing."*

"Don't you forget it!"

Salty turned and walked off the stage, leaving a silent Joe sitting on a high stool in the spotlight, blowing a slow plume of smoke into the dark. He made a poignant figure. He ought to play Salty's part. He'd be brilliant.

And Salty realized that was exactly what Joe had been doing with him! Joe had known exactly how to punch Salty's buttons. The play would be brilliant. Because of Joe.

And Felicia. They were two real pros. Joe had said she was the only one whose performance hadn't faltered.

Could Salty use his depressed rejection of her to make the audience believe he wanted Felicia? How could a man who knew he must relinquish a woman play a part in which he stalked her to keep her?

And he considered actors who hated each other, yet they could play lovers.

He didn't have to deal with revulsion. Quite the opposite. He had to deal with pretending to strive for her, when he was giving her up. All the stage actions were agony. It was what he wanted and couldn't have. What irony. What bitter irony.

The rehearsal on Saturday morning went okay. They ran right through at the right pace. Joe said, "You give me a little heart. I won't see you until Wednesday. We open on Friday. When you think of your part, think of it as a part of the whole. You are not a star, you are a part of the story."

Joe let them go. He was reluctant, he told them, but they'd tried hard enough to give him some courage.

So Salty and Felicia got to attend the party Salty was giving at his own house for his friends. Salty met Felicia's Aunt Helen, who was about thirty-three. She had big, limpid brown eyes with long cow lashes, and she didn't have much to say.

The invited men stayed, so that was a good indication of the caliber of women Emilie had gathered. Salty told her, "You know some nice women."

"Why does that surprise you?"

"You've been so hard-nosed with me."

"You know that Felicia is too young."

And he admitted it with great melancholy. "Yeah."

"So quit watching her like a hawk and let her flirt with some of your friends. You've got her locked in the kitchen, and she can't even cook."

"Did you neglect that part of her training so she wouldn't marry?"

"Cooking never caught her attention. She sets a beautiful table."

"Yeah."

"Salty, let her go."

He sighed, looked across the room and into the kitchen where Felicia was puttering around. "I have."

Emilie snorted. "No. You give no indication of letting go. You are so possessive of her, none of your friends can do more that sneak peeks at her."

"Emilie, I wish to God I'd seen you first, but I'm so zonked on her that I can't see any other woman."

"And you claim you're letting go of her?"

"Soon, now."

"You irritate me, Salty."

Sadly, he admitted, "I baffle me. I look at her and all she is is a rag, a bone and a hank of hair. She's made just like all women, but look at her."

"I do understand."

"She says she loves me."

Emilie frowned. "She told you so?"

"She's too young."

"Hold on to that thought."

"I can't be too rough about it until the play's done. She's perfect in it. You're in for a treat."

"It's her first major part. We're all going."

"One of the guys ask you?"

"Not there."

"Which one?"

"Henry."

Salty tilted his head back, trying to see why Henry would ask Emilie for a date, and why she would accept a date from Henry. Some people were just not suited. He told Emilie doubtfully, "Be patient. He'd be worth it."

She smiled a little. "But you question whether I would be?"

Salty said staunchly, "You're a sterling character."

Emilie laughed such a bubble of humor that Salty frowned at her for stepping out of her austere character. With her laugh, anyone would think she was a perfectly ordinary, open woman.

Salty abandoned Emilie to Henry, who wanted to know what Salty had said to make her laugh that way. While Emilie was teasing in her reply, Salty left them and went to the kitchen. He went for a drink of water, not because Peter had gone in to talk to Felicia.

He didn't get much water into his glass before he barged over and stood by Felicia so he could—visit with Peter.

He gave Peter a deadly look and asked, "Have you tried the hors d'oeuvres on the porch?" Three rooms away. Not subtle.

Peter smiled like a friend and replied, "I was looking at the confections in the kitchen." He grinned in a sharing humor.

Unhumored, Salty said a dead calm, "Go try those on the porch." That was clear enough.

Peter studied his friend and bobbed his head a couple of acknowledging times before he said softly, "Later." He lifted his brows and gave Felicia a quick look to allow his friend, Salty, to know he was trying to impress this budding woman.

Salty said, "Do you remember—" He looked at the corner of the ceiling. "It was June 2, 1955, and I had the fight with Colin P. Long?"

Peter nodded in a remembering way and commented reminiscently, "You murdered him. He lived, but not because you intended— You are a very strong man. I hear you."

Peter excused himself to find the hors d'oeuvres.

There were all kinds of food. The women guests had all brought something, and they steered males to taste their contributions for the feast.

Salty had barbecued ribs, made crisp perfect French fries, he had the perfect dressing for coleslaw and the

bread was homemade and marvelous. His offerings were
superb, but not necessarily female food. The women had
brought the goodies . . . and food, too.

Salty tried each of the contributed foods and knew he
could do better but, in this instance, he had to have food
the men would like; and he let the women shine with
their own table talents.

He was crafty. He never again left Felicia's side. Peter had spread the word almost instantly, but that didn't
stop Salty's possessiveness.

Emilie whispered to him a couple of trying times, "Let
up!"

Salty knew he should. He was startled and displeased
with his own conduct, but he couldn't seem to leave her
standing like a lone lamb in a room full of wolves.
His . . . friends. Not right then, they weren't.

And he saw that Tyrone was captured. Tyrone was
named for a handsome actor, but he'd taken after his
father. He was burly and being slicked down didn't hide
the fact that he was a reformed barroom fighter. He took
to the vapid-eyed Helen. Who could believe such a
combination?

But look at Salty and his own love. Look at Felicia,
who was any man's dream. And who was drawn to her?
Outside of all the others, he was. And he wasn't pretty.
He put his hand up to touch his left cauliflowered ear.
He wasn't good enough for her.

Felicia seemed to know exactly what he was thinking.
She leaned against his other arm, pulling it against her
round breast and said, "Let's sneak over to my house.
Everyone else is here."

His body reacted predictably. He said, "Shame on
you."

"We could leave the kids here. They're perfectly safe, and we could go...sailing?"

"I had no idea you were this wicked."

"You could be even more surprised." She smiled at him in such innocence. If it wasn't for her wicked rub against his arm, his ears probably wouldn't have gotten so red.

Bill came along and asked with smiling curiosity, "What's turned your ears so red?"

"She asked my age."

"A woman her age would do that." Bill smiled his Killer Smile at Felicia and asked, "You wanta get my ears red? I'm immune, but you could try."

That made Animal laugh. His real name was Terrance. His nickname was closer to the real him.

A feminine voice inquired, "Terrance! What kind of joke did he tell you to make you laugh that way?" She was Gloria.

Animal grinned and immediately lied. "He said I'm pretty."

Gloria looked at him soberly. "You've had a rough life at sea, but you have the most beautiful eyelashes I've ever seen."

He added, "I have curly hair, too."

Since he was bald, that did make Gloria drop her gaze down his body. She asked, "Did you shave your hair off?"

"I was just eighteen and at Guadalcanal."

Salty growled, "He got the Silver Star."

Terrance shrugged. "I thought I was dead, anyway, so I might as well go out fighting."

"How awful." Gloria shook her head, but her eyes stayed on Terrance.

He blushed and moved around and didn't know quite what to do next. So he punched Salty in the stomach.

What a rash thing to do, and he immediately realized it.

Salty caved in and said, "Help!" pitifully to Felicia. "He's mean."

She bravely put her body in front of Salty's and, unfortunately, laughed as she said, "You meany!"

Gloria scolded, "You never fight in the host's house."

Animal gasped, "I didn't know that."

Bob offered to Felicia, "I'll hold your coat." He looked down her dress and asked, "Your dress?" Then he smiled with undue humor at Salty.

Salty growled.

Emilie exclaimed, "I've never actually heard a man growl. Felicia, get away from him!"

Felicia laughed and gave Salty a very sassy look.

He controlled his smile enough and tried to look mean as he made a threatening throat sound. But that sort of sound wasn't for fist fighting, it was for another kind of tussle entirely.

All in all, the party was a great success. It launched a series of plans for getting together, from getting tickets and watching the Cleveland Indians play baseball, to renting a larger boat than Salty had and going on a cruise.

"We're sailors and we take to the water especially well." Bill was assuringly confident.

Emilie was the one who said, "We need to get tickets for the play next weekend."

Not surprisingly, none of his friends knew Salty was going to be in a play. They were so stimulated and amused that they couldn't think of language that would pass in that group. So they were animatedly silent.

Moving and exchanging glances and laughing, they were speechless.

The women counted noses and busily saw to it that they all paid up the money for Salty to get the tickets.

They would all be there. They would watch him stalk Felicia—and they would all know.

Hell, they all already knew.

Ten

Sunday was the day of rest. They went out on the boat. Mrs. T. consented to go along. She sat quietly, looked around and said nothing. They waited on her. The quasi-family sailed and sang and ate. Mrs. Thompson watched and listened. Salty found another cove, and they swam. Mrs. T. did not swim. She sat on the boat and watched. No, she observed.

The rocks were water smoothed, and the people wore sneakers to protect their toes.

The adults were like fish, but the kids splashed and swam underwater and were more like frogs.

The laughter was the nicest part for Mrs. Thompson. She didn't remember that people laughed so hard. And she saw the love Salty felt for Felicia. The tenderness. No man had ever shown such tenderness to Mrs. T.

She understood almost immediately that Salty thought he wasn't obvious. He couldn't not be obvious. He smiled at Felicia. He listened. He showed her things. And all the while he kept track of the children.

With reluctance, the selfish woman began to understand how it was between the two lovers. And she saw their serious problem. He was too old for Felicia. He knew it, but he couldn't help himself. He loved the young girl.

Mrs. T. narrowed her eyes. Did he realize how much Felicia loved him? That was the surprise. He was really a rather battered-looking man. He was gentle, but he'd been through a lot. It was obvious. Was his maleness what drew Felicia to him?

He was certainly male.

Silently, Mrs. Thompson studied the family. For the group *was* a family, whether they realized it or not. Felicia took as good care of the boys as Salty.

As they had lunch on board the silly boat, Mrs. T. asked Salty, "What was your given name?"

"Jerome."

She observed him. He went on eating, dismissing the name. "You traded a good name like that for... Salty?"

He looked up at her in a rather deadly way and said, "Yeah."

That's the way Salty would handle anything that annoyed him. He would choose sides and stick. Some time back, he'd left his real name behind. He was... Salty. Salty Brown. Jerome Brown would have been more elegant.

Actually, that's when Mrs. T. realized that Salty was elegant. That battered man had perfect manners.

"Why did you join the navy so young?"

"World War II started, and I had to help."

Mrs. T. considered him. How typically brief and to the point was his reply. "But you stayed in the navy."

"It suited me." Salty didn't encourage her questioning.

Mrs. T. thought Salty was one of the rare male types who liked travail. But it couldn't be between single people or even small groups, it had to be something impossible. A challenge.

That was probably why he wanted Felicia so much. Such a pairing was impossible. But if he ever did marry, he would be a good husband and a good father. Emilie was right. The two needed more privacy in order to decide...in order for Salty to realize he really had no choice at all.

As he maneuvered between boats to dock, Salty told Mrs. T. they had to go back to the city. "We—" he indicated Felicia and himself "—have to go to the theater this afternoon to practice our movements. We caught he—the dickens from Joe, the director, and we open Friday."

Mrs. T. eyed Salty suspiciously. He looked back at her. His look was bland, indifferent, patient endurance. She was not used to sailors and she took his word for it.

After docking, as they'd straightened up the boat and collected the debris, Felicia glanced at Salty a couple of times in a weighing manner. But she never said a word, nor did she question his words.

So the pair delivered the worn-out boys and a soothed and placid Mrs. T. back to their house; then Salty took Felicia to the empty Playhouse.

Even as he jimmied the lock on the door at the Playhouse stage entrance, she made no comment. She did note that his breathing was different. Her own picked up. She flicked the tip of her tongue along her lips.

Inside, he barred the door, even before he turned his head carefully and looked at her.

It was a stunning look. It was a primal look. What had women done, long ago, when there were no doors and a man had that need?

With Salty, Felicia felt only responding thrills, matching need.

Her lips parted and her big eyes were larger. He could drown in those eyes. He said hoarsely, "I want you."

She was equally intense. "I suspected."

There was no one else around. They had the whole place to themselves. He disrobed her. Slowly he unsheathed that body and looked at her. He breathed brokenly and he was so serious.

She didn't say a word. She looked back at him. She began to indicate that he was clothed and she was not. She picked at his shirt and made small gestures.

He rasped, "You do it."

Since he'd been so shocked the other time, she was more aware of her boldness and she fumbled.

He endured in a pitched sexual heat. He was intensely aware of her lightly touching hands, and he saw her self-consciousness. He loved it. She blushed. And even then, she tilted her head and peeked at him to be sure she had his attention.

She had it.

He had the smell of hot sex. He was a potent man and would continue to be so for the rest of his life. But now, it wasn't women he wanted, it was Felicia. Only she was his dream. His desire.

And he must let her go. She had a good, long life ahead of her. She needed to explore her acting talents. She was a superb actress. He could not tie her down to a man who was approaching middle age. It was 1962, and the whole world was out there just for her.

He loved her. Loved her? If he really loved her, he wouldn't have lured her here under false pretenses of rehearsal. What was he doing there with her? Why was he taking advantage of her crush in this way? He was adult, he had control, he could release her, leave her alone.

Soon. He would gently reject her soon, now. Not now, but soon. After the three-week run of the play. She was only intrigued with him. She didn't need his rejection at this time. Since he should continue for her sake and not upset her when she had this wonderful chance to show her talents, he would wait to release her from his hold.

Of course, if he did split up with her now, the poignancy she suffered would enhance her stage characterization.

S-s-shucks to that.

And a corner of his intensely involved mind noted that his struggle to clean up his nautical naughty words was becoming serious. His schooled tongue could control him even at this emotional time. He loved her.

He told her to stay put, then he searched the entire building. No one else was anywhere around. Then he took a plush, Victorian, curved fainting couch and set it stage center. And he put a soft spot on the couch.

He took her to the play's final scene, and they played it as it would have been played in private, in real life. He built them to that epic, emotional pitch; then he made love to her there in the empty theater. He made passionate love to her. He worshiped her, whom he knew he should not have.

He pretended she controlled him as he had his way with her. He was intensely gentle, sexual and very skilled. He drove her mad. His touches and sucklings were erotic and he sweat in sexual heat. His careful hands became more demanding and a little rougher.

She was a mass of impatient, writhing want.

He stretched it. He lifted her and carried her around to calm himself. It was a variation of the car-lifting calming. It was more exquisite for holding her, having her in his power, carrying her was thrilling to him.

She loved him.

He took her back to the couch...and he took her, driving them both wild.

When they were replete, she lay limp. Her hair was damp, and her sweaty, lubricated body was inert. He leaned on one elbow, curled by her side. His hard, male body was a sheen of sweat. His hair still shivered from his exhaustive efforts. His big, rough hand gently soothed her body. He looked at his love, and his hand followed his ardent gaze. He was her lover...for then.

She smiled lazily and reached a hand up to touch the hair that had fallen over his forehead. It was damp to her fingers. She said, "I love you."

He replied, "Yeah."

She said, "You are a great lover."

"It's all fantasy. I've dreamed of ending the play this way."

"I'm not sure we would be allowed to do it. This seduction lasted longer than all three acts."

"It just felt that way. Emotion slows or speeds things up. You are such a radically sensual female, it just seemed to take a long time. Actually, it was thirty-seven and a half seconds."

"If you know that, you were distracted."

"I always count, because I charge by the minute. Since you're a sex-hungry woman, you hurry things along. I feel used."

Helpless, she lay lax and her laughter was feeble. She shook her head. "I haven't the energy to laugh. Quit being funny."

"You're trying to get out of paying me."

"What am I supposed to pay?"

"A rain check."

And she laughed again. "You greedy man."

He took her into rigidly controlled arms, hugging her to his hot body and said only, "Yes."

But his voice wasn't teasing. It sounded...melancholy.

Her hand caressed his damp hair as her fingers gently combed it back. "You sound—sad. Are you disappointed I hurried you along so fast that you won't be paid?"

"Yeah." The word was soft and almost grieving.

"Have you had bad news?"

"No." He only had the knowledge that he must let her go. That wasn't news because he'd known it all along.

He moved slowly to get his jacket. He removed a slender tissue-wrapped package. It was the necklace of blue stones.

Salty put it around her throat and clasped it. Naked, wearing only his necklace, she got off the couch to find a mirror.

He watched her walk. He relished seeing her unclothed body move. And his necklace was her only artificial decoration. She came back to him and lay beside him.

It was an intimacy that was charmingly sweet. They spoke of their lives. As usual, he told stories in which he was the butt or the klutz or the blunderer.

She knew he lied. And she knew he was trying to withdraw from her. Their closely curled bodies were a lie. He wanted to leave her.

It was that knowledge which made the play a success. She knew he was rejecting her.

So did he.

Since she made no protest or accusation, he thought she was unknowing.

On opening night, the curtains parted, and Felicia was alone on the stage. The silence was potent. She was to begin with vocalized thoughts. She was to rise from the sofa at the back of the stage. She was wearing a long, sliplike flesh-colored satin that was shocking. She was to walk slowly forward and fiddle with stage props of flowers and books. She was to then turn as Salty came silently on stage. Her vocalized thinking would continue. He had no lines.

But she froze. She could not begin.

She sat and stared out over the footlights, and she could hear the minute sounds so she knew the seats were filled, and they were all waiting for her to speak. She could not.

Salty was instantly aware. And he knew she needed him.

She was, indeed, frozen.

Salty moved past the prompter and went too early onstage. He could hear the gasps of several behind him, but he heard Joe's sibilant, "Hush!" which silenced the soft exclamations.

With Salty's appearance, Felicia was triggered. She stood up and walked perfectly. As she spoke, her lines were even more poignantly true. The words were those of an abandoned woman who was lonely and needy.

The man the actress wanted wasn't there. But Felicia spoke to the man who was. It was stunning.

As the play progressed, the audience seemed not to breathe, they were so silent. The only breaks in the silence were the shattering applause on the closings of the curtains. The audience was so mesmerized by the play that there was no chatter as they waited for the next act. There were murmurs, there was a nervous cough or two, but the quiet from the audience was startling.

The play went on. The stalking of Felicia by Salty was riveting. His drawing the empathy from the audience was superb. They knew exactly what he felt. They felt it.

And when he finally cornered her and kissed her, the silence was pithy for that stunning kiss; then the applause was thunderous. It was astonishing. The kiss had to last longer so that their words could be heard when the kiss broke.

Felicia's tear-filled eyes looked back at Salty and she whispered, "I love you that much."

He held her and groaned.

The audience finally stilled, and the lovers were allowed to say their words and continue with the plot. And when the disaster was averted and the villain finally caught, Felicia asked through all the exchange of police and the people who'd been trapped, "Where is he? Where is Leon? Has anyone seen Leon?"

The others brushed off her questions distractedly, saying they didn't know, they hadn't seen him. And they went frenzied about contacting others and leaving hurriedly. Finally, only Felicia was onstage.

As the last one left, Felicia put her frantic hands in her hair and screamed in her deep, dramatic voice a hopeless, "Where's Leon? What has happened to Leon!"

It was a soul-touching cry.

She went to the phone on the far left of the stage, scrambled her fingers through a telephone book and dialed the number, before she stood, her face to the ceiling, her back to the audience.

The muffled replying voice sound could be heard by the silent audience. Then Felicia shouted, "Where is Leon? What has happened to him?"

And offstage Salty's voice echoed her words, "Where are you? Where *are* you! Answer me!"

Her body stiffened, she dropped the phone and turned so that her back was still to the audience. She gasped. And her sound went through every tense body in the audience.

Salty came onstage from the right wing. He hesitated as their eyes sought any harm to the other, then they slowly advanced to meet stage center. They were leaning forward, so intense. Their hands touched. And finally he gathered her to him in the most tenderly controlled violence ever seen.

And the two kissed as slowly, slowly, the curtains closed.

It was devastating. The audience stood up and cheered as their eyes spilled, and they laughed and responded thunderously. It was an emotional lemon squeeze.

It was like that every night. The word spread that Joe had a real live hit, and tickets were scalped. The prices people were willing to pay shocked the charity backers. They wanted the full price of the tickets. They begged Joe to get his cast to do the play just two more times.

Joe consulted the amateur volunteer cast, and they agreed. It was so marvelous to be in such a hit that they were exuberant. Salty and Felicia exchanged a communicating look before they quietly agreed.

The play was an ordeal for them. Salty's soul was lost to a pre-woman who didn't need an old sailor as an iron anchor around her neck. She needed to be free to fly

with this great opportunity. The publicity the hit garnered was superb for such a fledgling actress. It was
priceless.

She was.

So each night they went through their ordeal. The
tension never faltered. They played strained lovers on the
stage, then continued it offstage.

Salty was more finely honed. He looked as if he suffered. And Felicia was a haunted, big-eyed, any man's
dream in that flesh-colored satin sliplike gown. Her wavy
dark hair was loose and those big, haunting eyes had
such impact. Her rich voice went into the souls of those
who watched. The combination of the two was power-
ful.

Offstage it wasn't any better. It was worse. And he
knew that Felicia knew he was withdrawing from her.

Joe told Salty. "Your lover's quarrel made the play a
winner. I've never seen such acting. Could you two make
up and still carry the play that way? Or would you have
to quarrel every time to get the right edge?"

"Go to hell!"

Salty didn't mean for Joe to actually do that, he just
wanted to grieve without anybody needing explanations
or chitchat.

Mrs. T. evaluated Salty and was drawn by his suffering. When would anyone think Mrs. Thompson could be
compassionate for a man's suffering? It was the talk of
all the women who knew her. And of course, Mrs. T.
was one of Emilie's friends, and therefore an "aunt" to
Felicia.

But it was Salty who garnered Mrs. T.'s empathy. She
thought Felicia was too young for Salty. She was. No
doubt about it. But Mrs. T. thought Felicia should have
Salty for a couple of years, then get divorced and get

back on the stage before she found a younger man. One who was more suitable.

In that turbulent time, Mrs. T. mentioned all of her thoughts to Emilie on the phone.

Emilie replied, "Felicia's regard is for all of her life. No other man will catch her attention."

"Does Salty realize that?"

"I've told him to leave her alone."

Mrs. T. had the gall to say, "You ought not interfere in other people's lives."

"Felicia interfered in mine. My sister gave me her new baby and told me to care for her."

Mrs. T. guessed, "You hate the child and regret having to cope for her?"

"No. I was just giving you an example."

"And that man who wanted you to give Felicia away. You still want him?"

Emilie retorted, "No. That was so shocking that I knew he wasn't the man I thought he was."

"So?"

"I haven't found a Salty."

"Good God! You want *Salty?*"

Impatiently, Emilie replied, "No. Someone . . . like him."

"There are all of his friends. Did any of them measure up?"

"No. I suspect no man ever will."

So then Mrs. Thompson found a time to tell Salty, "Emilie needs a good man." With that pronouncement, Mrs. T. then clasped her hands in front of her and settled her shoulders as if she'd just given an edict.

Salty gave that some distracted thought and called his late friend George's brother, Samuel. He told Sam, "There's a woman here you ought to look at."

"I've looked at enough women and I don't want to have to look at any more. If there's really a God, I'll be old enough pretty soon, I won't need one. They're all leeches."

"This one's different. She'll test you."

Sam was idle and indifferent. "Yeah? In bed?"

"Probably that, too, but she'll see if you're an iron man or if you're hollow."

"Uh . . . Maybe. I'll think about it."

Salty was distracted. "You do that. You can stay here with us."

"Us?"

Salty sighed and expanded it. "I've adopted three boys, and there's an old witch who lives in and doesn't do anything."

"Just that sounds interesting. Why's she there with you?"

His voice was a rasp. "She'd call the doctor or the police if either was needed."

"Yeah. Hmm. I may come by. I'll let you know. I've missed your abrasiveness."

With some impatience with the lengthening call, Salty was a little snide with his dead friend's brother. "I love you, too. Get your butt up here."

"This woman after you?"

"No."

His interest caught, Sam observed, "No accounting for taste. If she doesn't like you, she won't like me. We're revoltingly similar."

"That's why I called you."

"You got a hankering for her?" Why should he have snapped that out so fast?

With the patience the situation called for, Salty explained, "I got tangled up with a nymph. Emilie is her adopted aunt without being much older. Emilie is in her early thirties. She's a good-looking woman and she's a survivor. She was in the underground in France during the war."

"Wow. She can probably handle me."

Salty's words were sure. "She could."

"I haven't come to see you because, you know, it's tough to remember George."

"Yeah."

"I'll call you."

Salty waved the bait, "The Animal is after her."

"Him?"

"Yeah. And Curt. Larry—"

Sam decided, "I'll be there ... this weekend."

"I'll get tickets for you for the play."

"You doing that, again?" Sam wasn't too surprised.

"Yeah."

Sam chuckled, "I'd probably come just to see you strut your stuff."

"This one is serious."

Sam laughed.

At noon, Felicia came into Salty's house. She was excessively quiet. She looked at him with haunted eyes. "Are you going to marry me and live happily ever after?"

He was positive that he should wait to make the break with her for her sake. When he did reject her, no matter how careful he was, she was going to suffer. He already knew what his own anguish would be. He said, "You need to be older. You need to go to school. We'll be friendly for a time."

"How friendly?"

"Like now." And he silently groaned as he took her against him.

But they rarely had private time. The boys were drawn to her. They laughed and touched her, but both big boys felt too mature to sit on her lap. They did hug her and they allowed her to kiss them. John sat on her lap.

It was just a good thing he loved the boys as much as he did or he'd have been selfish about sharing her with them.

He told Felicia, "I've asked my friend Sam to visit. He's coming for the play this weekend. Do you think Emilie would be kind enough to sit with him?"

"You could ask her."

So Salty called Emilie, and she said she wouldn't mind.

Salty hung up the phone and felt that he'd done all he had to do.

Through the run, the cast members were given two tickets to each performance. At first, Salty had given his away. The play wasn't really what his friends generally attended, but they'd all been eager to see this one . . . for Salty's support. But they lied. They'd read the reviews and they knew the play was—special. Then they'd talked among themselves.

When his friends started badgering him for more tickets, he encouraged them to buy their own. And he returned his to the ticket booth so the charity could get the money.

Emilie had already seen the play once. She knew its impact. And she would go to see it again. That said a good deal about the play, or her curiosity, or her love for Felicia. Which was it?

Actually, it was the offer of a man Salty had specifically chosen to present to her for her selection. Emilie was curious.

So, Sam came to visit. And Sam blinked over the magic of Felicia and was silent. He recognized the anguished indecision in Salty. And Sam met Emilie. He took her to the play, and she sitting next to him distracted him from the play.

With that final performance, the play was done.

It was time for Salty to give up Felicia. He was determined that she have the chance to be free of him.

The next day, Felicia came over to Salty's for lunch as if there was no Armageddon looming. She kissed him and called him Leon. He snarled a rasp and said the name was a sissy one.

She retorted, "He was a good and brave man, and so are you. You're a man to take life and live it boldly. Small worries or events are brushed aside." Her stony gaze challenged him.

"This is as good a time as any, Felicia. I'm leaving town. The boys and I are moving."

She was appalled. "Where are we going?"

Of all the reactions, he had never expected this prewoman to be such a sticker burr. He groaned and shook his head.

She asked, "We're going to become bums and hitchhike? Go wherever some truck takes us? Will that be good for the kids at this age?"

"Felicia—don't."

"Don't?" Tears clung to her bottom lashes in spite of her intense, silent command that they disappear.

Salty's rasp was rough. "Don't make this hard for me."

"I've become quite good at making things hard for you. Why would you want me to stop now?"

"I have to leave you."

"Your wives are catching up with you? You have other commitments? Is there something you've been keeping to yourself as you used me and toyed with me?"

He groaned from his soul and turned his head. There, in the doorway were three very serious little boys. He stared at them as they returned his stare.

Felicia sat down rather abruptly, her trembling knees no longer reliable. She shivered and wrapped her arms around herself.

Rod asked seriously, "We're leaving Cleveland?"

Salty replied kindly, "I needed to tell Felicia first."

"Yeah."

The two younger boys were silent. Their serious glances went from one adult to the other.

Salty told them, "We'll talk later. I need to speak with Felicia right now."

Rod replied, "No. We want to hear. This is about us, too. We need to know."

How many times had Salty used that expression? How many times had he told the boys, "You need to know."

Salty said to the boys, "I'm sorry."

Rod was sure, "We need to hear."

Salty asked her permission, "Felicia?"

And her marvelous voice was guttural as she responded with, "They are a part of me."

Then the boys went to Felicia. Rod and Mike stood on either side of her and picked up her hands, while John leaned on her knees with his arm across them in a very protective stance.

They faced Salty quite seriously. And that isolated figure saw the tears roll down Felicia's cheeks.

"My love," he began.

But she interrupted, "If I truly am your love, then you will marry me."

And the boys nodded. Rod said, "Yes."

"Felicia, I'm too old for you."

Rod replied, "You do okay."

Mike said, "Yeah."

John asked Felicia, "How old are you?"

Felicia said, "A hopeless hundred years old, today."

Salty groaned.

John asked Rod in a steaming hiss, "Is Dad *over* a hundred?"

Rod said, "No. He's piling it on."

Felicia agreed, "Every time."

Salty began, "I'm twenty years older—"

Felicia warned, "If I hear that one more time, I'm going to scream! Then you can try to think of some sort of explanation for the neighbors before the police get here."

His temper began to rise. "I was trying to do this tactfully—"

She shouted, "What's *tactful* about rejecting me?"

"You'll find a nice young man—"

Stridently, she retorted, "I don't want a 'nice young man,' I want you!"

Rod said, "Yeah." Just like Salty, except his voice was clear.

Salty asked the boys, "Do you mean you want Felicia for your mother?"

While the two little ones nodded in serious, exaggerated ups and downs of their heads, Rod said, "No, she wants to marry you and be your wife and sleep with you in your bed."

Felicia was curious, "How'd you know that?"

"That's what Skinny's second mother wanted. He heard her say it to his dad."

"Did they get married?"

"No, but he married the next one."

Salty watched his feet move, and he finally said, "I guess I'd better marry you."

"How kind."

Salty explained, "I just don't have the years to try to find someone similar." Then he looked at her in some despair.

"You like me?" She raised her eyebrows.

"I meant similar... to me. You're very different."

She was grim. "I'll keep you stimulated."

"Then you'll marry me?"

"I thought you'd never ask."

Among their friends, it was the wedding of the year. It was a wonderful party that got a little raucous, but all the neighbors were there so no one complained.

It wasn't long after that when Emilie and Sam were married. Salty gave the bride away. And there was another party that lasted three days. Sam said he'd never had a chance to escape.

It was true. While Salty claimed all the credit for Sam and Emilie's marriage, seeing the play had been a remarkable basis for a beginning courtship. They were—suckered in. Their shields of self-protection were weakened by the emotion of the play, and the two strangers had become gentle with each other.

At first, it was the play. But between Sam and Emilie it gradually became sincere desire, then intense desire before they really fell in love. The play had just helped them get over the awkward beginnings and hurried them on a little.

There were more marriages in 1962 than ever before in Cleveland's history. Salty checked that later, and statistics said, "Naw. It was just about like any other year."

It had just been the people they knew. All were marriageable age, and they'd all loyally been to the play.

The Browns bought a house on the south edge of Temple, a small town just south of Cleveland. The house was a deserted old wreck, but the ten acres were good, and there was a leaning barn that looked just right to house chickens. All sailors talk about having chicken farms.

Felicia got to redo the entire house and open some rooms out and close some in. It cost more than building a whole new house. But Felicia had such a wonderful time of it that the money was well spent.

The three boys took a while to adjust. There was so much room. But there were Salty and Felicia's take-in kids, and the waifs they harbored. There were the adopted ones and five of their own making, so the place bulged with kids and games and fights and laughter.

Felicia had chosen well. A man chases a woman until she catches him.

* * * * *

Take 4 bestselling love stories FREE

Plus get a FREE surprise gift!

Special Limited-time Offer

Mail to Silhouette Reader Service™

3010 Walden Avenue
P.O. Box 1867
Buffalo, N.Y. 14269-1867

YES! Please send me 4 free Silhouette Desire® novels and my free surprise gift. Then send me 6 brand-new novels every month, which I will receive months before they appear in bookstores. Bill me at the low price of $2.44 each plus 25¢ delivery and applicable sales tax, if any.* That's the complete price and—compared to the cover prices of $2.99 each—quite a bargain! I understand that accepting the books and gift places me under no obligation ever to buy any books. I can always return a shipment and cancel at any time. Even if I never buy another book from Silhouette, the 4 free books and the surprise gift are mine to keep forever.

225 BPA ANRS

Name	(PLEASE PRINT)	
Address	Apt. No.	
City	State	Zip

This offer is limited to one order per household and not valid to present Silhouette Desire® subscribers. *Terms and prices are subject to change without notice.
Sales tax applicable in N.Y.

UDES-94R   ©1990 Harlequin Enterprises Limited

Rugged and lean...and the best-looking, sweetest-talking men to be found in the entire Lone Star state!

Diana Palmer

LONG, TALL TEXANS

In July 1994, Silhouette is very proud to bring you Diana Palmer's first three LONG, TALL TEXANS. CALHOUN, JUSTIN and TYLER—the three cowboys who started the legend. Now they're back by popular demand in one classic volume—and they're ready to lasso your heart! Beautifully repackaged for this special event, this collection is sure to be a longtime keepsake!

"Diana Palmer makes a reader want to find a Texan of her own to love!"
          —Affaire de Coeur

LONG, TALL TEXANS—the first three— reunited in this special roundup!

Available in July, wherever Silhouette books are sold.

LTT

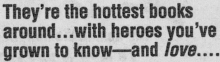

SILHOUETTE® *Desire*®

Big Bad WOLFE

WOLFE WATCHING
by Joan Hohl

Undercover cop Eric Wolfe knew *everything* about divorcée Tina Kranas, from her bra size to her bedtime—without ever having spent the night with her! The lady was a suspect, and Eric had to keep a close eye on her. But since his binoculars were getting all steamed up from watching her, Eric knew it was time to start wooing her....

WOLFE WATCHING, Book 2 of Joan Hohl's devilishly sexy Big Bad Wolfe series, is coming your way in July...only from Silhouette Desire.

IT'S OUR 1000TH SILHOUETTE ROMANCE, AND WE'RE CELEBRATING!

JOIN US FOR A SPECIAL COLLECTION OF LOVE STORIES BY AUTHORS YOU'VE LOVED FOR YEARS, AND NEW FAVORITES YOU'VE JUST DISCOVERED. JOIN THE CELEBRATION...

April
REGAN'S PRIDE by Diana Palmer
MARRY ME AGAIN by Suzanne Carey

May
THE BEST IS YET TO BE by Tracy Sinclair
CAUTION: BABY AHEAD by Marie Ferrarella

June
THE BACHELOR PRINCE by Debbie Macomber
A ROGUE'S HEART by Laurie Paige

July
IMPROMPTU BRIDE by Annette Broadrick
THE FORGOTTEN HUSBAND by Elizabeth August

SILHOUETTE ROMANCE...VIBRANT, FUN AND EMOTIONALLY RICH! TAKE ANOTHER LOOK AT US! AND AS PART OF THE CELEBRATION, READERS CAN RECEIVE A FREE GIFT!

YOU'LL FALL IN LOVE ALL OVER AGAIN WITH SILHOUETTE ROMANCE!

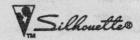

CEL1000